SCOUT'S HONOR

AND THE CAVE OF COURAGE

SCOUT'S HONOR
AND THE CAVE OF COURAGE

ANNA LEVINE

PJ Library, a program of the Harold Grinspoon Foundation
67 Hunt Street, Suite 100
Agawam, MA 01001
U.S.A.

PJ Our Way™ is an unregistered trademark of the Harold Grinspoon Foundation.

Visit us on the web at www.hgf.org and www.pjourway.org

Book design and cover illustration by Tim Palin Creative

First Edition

10 9 8 7 6 5 4 3 2 1

Printed in the United States of America

To my *chaverim* in Hashomer Hatzair,
for friendships that last a lifetime.

Special thanks to Gidi Bashan at the
Jewish National Fund (JNF) for guiding
me through the caves at the
Adullam Nature Reserve.

CHAPTER 1

"It's too bad the airline lost your baggage," said Amit to his cousins as they walked into his room.

"No big deal," said Josh. He pretended not to care, but privately he felt rotten. The camping equipment he and his twin brother, Nate, had packed was on its way to Australia.

Nate shrugged. "I heard about a guy who sued the airline for losing his bag."

"Really?" said Amit. "What happened?"

"He lost his case."

It took a second before Amit groaned.

Josh rolled his eyes. "Get used to it," he said.

Amit tossed each of his cousins a set of Scouts beige shirts and pants. "Good thing my brothers kept their old uniforms," he said. "And we can share my gear."

"Thanks," said Josh, pulling on the pants. This was their first trip to Israel, and Josh wanted everything to go right. "Time to reconnect with family," his mother had said. "And have an adventure. A Scouts trip with Amit will do both at once."

"These are a little big for me," said Josh.

"Here's my brother's belt," said Amit.

"He won't mind if I borrow it?"

"Better check with him first," said Nate. "You heard about the belt that was arrested."

"Arrested," said Amit. "Why?"

"Because he held up a pair of pants!"

Amit laughed.

Nate tried on the other pair of pants. "These'll do. But the pockets feel empty. I wish I had my flashlight."

"Tell me about it," said Josh. "I had big plans for my Swiss Army knife."

"I have an extra flashlight somewhere," said Amit. "And we need to go to the store to buy some snacks before it closes."

Stifling a yawn, Josh tried to shake off his grogginess. Traveling into a different time zone made him feel like his body had arrived but his head was still floating somewhere above the Atlantic Ocean. According to the plane monitor, they had flown 5,683 miles. That was the distance from JFK airport in New York to Tel Aviv, Israel, not counting the twisty car ride from the airport to Jerusalem once they'd landed.

"Hey, Josh, if you're too tired to go, you can stay here," said Amit. "Nate can come with me."

Josh shook his head. "Tired? Who said I was tired? I'm not going to spend my winter vacation sleeping!"

Josh stepped out of the house behind his twin and cousin and stood in the cool Jerusalem evening. The streets were full of dog walkers, cyclists and cars that zipped in and out of lanes at daring speeds. Josh swerved as a cyclist raced past him.

"Here we are," said Amit, holding the store door open.

They squeezed inside. From floor to ceiling there was no unused inch of space. Stacked one on top of the other, cans of tuna, boxes of spaghetti, bottles of ketchup, mustard, mayonnaise, and all kinds of sandwich spreads lined the shelves.

"Hi, Eli," said Amit to the man behind the counter. "These are my twin cousins from America."

"Twins?" said Eli, peering over the top of his newspaper. "How do people tell you apart?"

"He's the evil twin," said Nate.

"And you're the stunt double?" said Eli.

Nate laughed.

Josh was glad the shopkeeper hadn't mentioned the birthmark on his forehead, which was how most people told them apart.

Eli stuck out his hand. A miniature blob wrapped in colored foil rested in his palm.

"What's that?" asked Josh.

"A Krembo. It's a kind of sweet found only in Israel. Sold only in winter."

"A winter candy?" said Nate, as Josh reached out to take it.

"Careful!" shouted Amit.

Too late, the candy collapsed in Josh's palm.

"What happened?" asked Josh. He tried to push the candy back into shape, but it was totally squished.

Eli's laugh resounded through the pea-sized room. "You have to be careful how you hold it," he said. He held up another Krembo. "They're as delicate as people. On the outside, they look big and strong, but touch them roughly, and – poof! – all that remains is an empty shell." Eli smiled at Josh.

"I see," said Josh, feeling a bit unnerved.

"We're done," said Amit. He set the supplies on the counter. "Mom will come and pay you tomorrow."

"Fine," said Eli. "You boys have a great time."

As they left the store, Nate fell into step beside Josh. "That Eli was kind of strange, wasn't he?"

Josh nodded. "Everything here feels a bit weird."

"Hey, Josh," said Nate, as he elbowed him in the ribs. "I'm glad the airline didn't ship you to Australia with our suitcases!"

Josh shoved his brother back. Though there were moments when Nate could be really annoying, Josh wouldn't want to go anywhere without him.

CHAPTER 2

The next morning, Aunt Tamar dropped off the boys at Scout headquarters. The entrance was cluttered with crates of food, thermoses, logs, and lengths of rope.

"Gabi," Aunt Tamar called, beckoning to a broad-shouldered boy with curly brown hair. "These are my nephews. It's their first time in Israel. Keep an eye on them, okay?"

"Of course," said Gabi, climbing over a pile of logs to meet Josh and Nate. "Amit's been very excited about your joining us. I'll introduce you to the rest of the group once everyone gets here." He turned to Aunt Tamar. "Don't worry about a thing."

"Have fun, boys," said their aunt. "Josh, Nate, I'll call your mom and tell her you're fine."

Josh took a step closer to his brother. Together they eyed the Scouts gathering in the parking lot, shouting greetings to each other in Hebrew.

"Sure doesn't sound like the Hebrew we hear in synagogue," said Nate. "I can't understand a word."

"And that's not the only weird thing," Josh whispered. "What's with all the girls? What kind of trip will this be if girls are with us?"

Nate shrugged. "I'm sure the girls have their own group."

Whenever Amit visited the boys in New York, it was easy for him to fit in with their friends because he could speak English. But now that Josh and Nate were with Amit in Israel, Josh realized there was going to be a serious language problem.

"Don't worry about the Hebrew," said Amit, over-hearing the boys. "Most of my friends speak English. Like Tomer." Amit waved to a thin, dark-skinned boy with a big smile.

"Hi, Josh. Hi, Nate." Tomer paused. "Or should I say 'Hi, Nate. Hi, Josh.' Amit told me all about you, even how to tell you apart." He glanced from Nate to Josh and then back again, his brown eyes sizing them up.

Josh quickly brushed his hair forward to cover his birth mark.

"Hey, anyone see Microscope?" someone shouted.

Tomer groaned. "That's Roy. He's impossible to get rid of and even harder to ignore."

Nate and Josh eyed the kid with the sweatband around his forehead. He was wearing a Scout uniform that looked like it had shrunk a few too many times.

"There you are, Microscope," said Roy, waving. "Almost missed you."

Josh gave Tomer a puzzled look. "Microscope?"

"Roy's nickname for me. He says I'm so small you can't see me without one."

"Oh." Josh wondered what Roy might call him. Roy was thin and gawky, with hair that stuck out from his head as if he'd been in the spin cycle for too long. As Josh turned to ask Amit if Roy was going to be with them the whole time, something wet and hard hit him, smack on the side of the head. It was an olive pit and the soggy remains of the fruit.

"Bull's eye!" shouted Roy. He stuck another olive in his mouth, ate the fruit, and got the pit ready for spitting. "Hey Gingies, your red hair makes a perfect target." Roy aimed the pit at Nate, who ducked.

"Not funny," said Amit.

One of the girls giggled. "Are those twins your cousins?" she asked Amit. "I've got identical twin cousins too. Shauna is the quiet, shy one." Looking at Nate, she smiled, showing more braces than she had teeth. Then she took a piece of chocolate from her pocket and offered it to him. "If you need me to translate, just let me know."

"Thanks, Dana," said Amit. "But we all know enough English to get by."

"Duck!" yelled Nate, pushing Dana out of the way as Roy spit another olive pit at them.

"Don't worry about Roy," Dana said to Nate. "He's like a sheep in wolf's clothing." She picked up a pit and aimed it at Roy. "Get lost," she said.

"What d'you call a lost wolf?" asked Nate, keeping an eye out for flying olive pits.

"What?" said Dana.

"A where-wolf," said Nate.

Dana laughed. "Except we always know where Roy is."

"What does Gingie mean?" asked Josh.

"From ginger, which means redhead," Dana translated. "But your color's more like copper."

"It makes it easy for us to find each other," said Nate.

Which was a good thing, thought Josh. He didn't want to lose sight of his brother in this crowd, where everyone was dressed the same: beige pants, hiking boots, beige kerchiefs tied around their necks, and backpacks slung over their shoulders.

Gabi unfolded a checklist. "Roll call," he said. "Roy, Tomer, Amit, Sari, Dana, Nate, and Josh."

"All present," said Amit and Roy.

"And accounted for," added Tomer.

Dana and Sari cheered. "We're here!"

"Dana?" said Josh. "Sari?"

"Don't you have girls in America?" asked Dana.

"In America, the boys' and girls' Scout groups are separate," said Nate.

"No wonder you wanted to join us," said Dana. "You'll see. It's more fun being together."

As Gabi organized packing the bags and equipment onto the bus, he introduced Josh and Nate to some of the other kids and counselors. "When we arrive I'll show you how to set up the best campsite ever. I'm a knot-tying, hammock-making, fire pit-digging expert."

Roy snorted. "I know how to do all that stuff."

"Then you'll be a great helper." Gabi turned to Josh and Nate. "Are you two up for exploring some tunnels and caves?"

Josh and Nate nodded. "Sure thing," they said.

"That's the attitude I'm looking for," said Gabi.

Once everything had been stored at the bottom of the bus, Amit sprinted for the door. "Come on!" he shouted from the window. "We're leaving."

The driver revved the engine, and the bus belted out a cloud of exhaust. Josh coughed and hurried toward the door, sliding into the empty seat Nate had saved for him.

Josh tried to remember the names of the Scouts from the other groups Gabi had introduced them to earlier. Noah, the blond kid, talking to Shimon with the shaggy hair cut. Daniel and Nimrod sitting in front. The girls,

Miriam and Leah, sitting a few seats behind him. Dror and Tzach, which were hard names to say, sitting in the very back.

Josh fidgeted in his seat. He stared ahead trying to ignore his jumpy stomach. He could become a new, more courageous Josh here, since no one but Amit and Nate knew him from before.

"Are you feeling okay?" asked Nate.

"I'm good," said Josh. "Don't worry." He didn't want to ruin things for Nate like he had on their last Scout trip. Sure, he hadn't known that he had a fever until they reached home. But everyone saw how Nate had to carry Josh's backpack to the campsite. Then, when everyone was picked for baseball teams, Josh was picked last and was the first to strike out. Josh sat up straighter. This trip was an opportunity to prove himself and make a new first impression.

The last person to board the bus was an athletic-looking guy. He had closely cropped hair and wore a green shirt, not the Scouts' beige. As the man turned, Josh noticed a black strap across his shoulder and a long, thin barrel hanging down toward his knees.

Josh froze. The man was armed, and they were sitting at point-blank range!

"Quick!" cried Josh, grabbing Nate by the collar of his shirt and shoving him to the floor. "That man's got a gun!"

CHAPTER 3

Amit leaned over his cousins' seat. "Hey, what're you doing down on the floor?"

Josh looked up at Amit's puzzled frown. The blood rushed to his face.

Nate pushed Josh off him. "My brother's testing his reflexes. You know, practicing how to dodge bullets."

Amit laughed. "You're quick."

"What's he planning on shooting?" asked Josh, climbing back up to his seat.

"Hopefully nothing," said Amit. "On every trip there has to be a guide who carries a gun. It's the law."

"The law?" said Nate.

"To keep us safe."

Josh tried swallowing, but couldn't. There was a huge lump in his throat. "How about where we're going?" he croaked. "It's safe there, right?"

"I think the place was used as a hideout from Roman soldiers. The Jews dug ramparts beneath the ground with tunnels and caves. When they were in danger, they'd crawl inside and out of sight." Amit looked out the window. "I don't think we'll find many Roman soldiers lurking around anymore."

Josh forced a laugh. "They're history now, right?"

Amit punched him on the arm. "Yeah, ancient history."

The bus pulled out of the parking lot. The Scouts cheered. Nate joined a card game with Amit and Tomer. Josh pretended to be interested in the scenery outside the window. Despite Amit's reassurance that it was all ancient history, Josh wasn't convinced. At home, the bus shelters were made of glass to keep out the wind, rain and snow. Here, they looked like they were made of thick concrete, to protect against bullets.

The bus driver swung underneath the highway onto a side road. Josh steadied himself. Fresh air blew in through the open windows. The sun was shining as if it were the middle of August and not December.

Gabi had told Josh about exploring the tunnels and caves. Josh had never been in anything narrower than the kitchen broom closet. What if he crawled into one of the caves, got stuck, and couldn't find his way out?

The churning feeling in his stomach grew stronger as they drove farther and farther away from the city.

Finally the bus lurched to a stop.

"Everyone out!"

Josh was the last to step off the bus, almost colliding with his brother, who was standing in front of him.

"Move," said Josh.

Nate stayed put as if he'd been hammered into the ground like a tent peg. "Look!" he said.

Josh peered over his brother's shoulder. There was nothing to see. Hardly a shrub. Not even a tree to pee behind, or a rolling field of green grass for soccer. Instead, a part-rocky, part-brambly, part-terraced stretch of land spread out in front of them as far as the eye could see. "Probably just a pit stop," said Josh.

"You got the pit part right," said Nate.

"Welcome to Adullam Park," said Gabi. "It may not appear like much at first glance, but there are water cisterns, mazes of tunnels, and burial caves beneath us."

"Burial caves?" said Josh.

"Buried bones," said Roy.

"In biblical times," explained Gabi, "Joshua led the Israelites into the ancient land of Israel, where he conquered this area, taking it from King Adullam. Lots of wars happened in these parts." Gabi took a long look around. "This is the Elah Valley, where they say that the young King David fought Goliath."

"Get outta here!" said Nate. "For real?"

Roy butted in. "And a thousand years after David and Goliath, these caves were used by Bar Kochba and his army to escape the Romans. My mother's boyfriend, Baruch, told me all about this place. He said a whole bunch of tunnels run underground where skeletons have been found." Roy turned to Josh, "Skeletons with their heads lopped off."

"They were decapitated?" Josh asked.

"Whooooooosh!" said Roy, whipping a stick through the air. "All it takes is one sharp slice. If you don't believe me, call Baruch. Ask him, he'll tell you."

Nate jumped out of the way as the stick whipped by him. "Hey, Roy, you know why skeletons don't fight each other, right?"

Roy stopped waving the stick and shrugged.

"They don't have the guts," said Nate.

Tomer slapped his left leg, then his right one and gave two thumbs-up.

Amit laughed.

"Watch that stick, Roy," said Gabi. "I don't want any heads rolling around here." Gabi draped his arm over Roy's shoulder. "I'm glad to hear you're getting to know Baruch. I've met him, and he's a good guy. He was a Scout, too."

Roy snorted. "He's okay, except when he starts acting like he's my father. I hate that."

"I know what you mean..." Gabi paused awkwardly for a moment, then changed the subject. "Okay, so a bit more about this place. Many of the tunnels have been sealed off to be reconstructed and made safer for tourists. None of you are allowed to go in them. Got that?"

"But we aren't tourists," said Roy, shrugging off Gabi's arm. "We're Scouts." He slapped Josh on the back. "Right, Gingie?"

Josh grimaced. "Right," he said.

"Right," said Gabi. "We're responsible Scouts. Tomorrow we're going to Beit Govrin, where we'll have a guided tour through some of the tunnels."

"Guided tours are for wimps." Roy groaned. "And tourists who don't know how to rough it."

Gabi made a V with his index and middle finger. He pointed it toward his eyes and then at Roy's. "You can't explore the tunnels without me. Got it?"

"Got it," said Roy.

"That goes for you too, Josh," said Gabi.

Josh nodded. "Sure thing." He tried to change the subject. "I like your badge."

"It's not just any badge, Josh. This is the Scout's lily. It's special because of the Star of David behind it. You have to earn it."

"Earn it?"

"Prove you're Israeli Scout-worthy. You can start by taking care of these." Gabi pulled nine Hanukkah candles and a box of matches from his backpack. He handed them to Josh.

"Here," he said. "Eight candles and the shammash to light them. Tomorrow is the last night of Hanukkah. We're going to build a big campfire and light a Hanukkah menorah. Your job is to keep these candles from getting lost and broken."

Roy burst into laughter. "A big job for a little guy! Babysitting Hanukkah candles."

"Knock it off, Roy," said Gabi. "Scouts are supposed to be welcoming and helpful. Let's show some team spirit."

Josh felt his face grow hot. Roy was right. It was the kind of job you gave to somebody who looked like they couldn't do anything else. They were standing at the very place where the Jewish hero Joshua won great battles, David slew Goliath and heroes showed super-human courage. Now Josh was here too – to babysit Hanukkah candles.

Josh bit his lip. He'd show Roy. He'd show Gabi. He'd show them all that he could be more than just a candle holder. He only needed the right opportunity.

CHAPTER 4

"This is the perfect spot," said Gabi. "Everyone pick up a log and a piece of rope and come here. We'll start with the clove hitch."

They lugged their logs to where Gabi was sitting and joined him in a circle, ropes in hand.

"This is the knot that'll get you started. Once you master this one we can build a bench and a table and have our own little zoolah."

"Zoolah?" said Nate.

"Campsite," said Dana.

"Hangout," said Amit.

"'Knot' a bad idea," said Nate.

Gabi groaned. "Okay, everyone, hold the rope in your right hand. This is called the running end. Take it and throw it halfway over the log. Now make an X by winding it around the log a second time. Push the running end upwards underneath the X and pull it tight. Presto! The clove hitch."

Josh looked down at the knot he'd made and then at Gabi's. Josh's knot was perfect. "Now what?"

"Now we lash the logs to the trees to make benches."

"Lash?" said Nate.

"Like this." Gabi took Josh's log and told him to hold

it against the tree. Nate held the other end of the log while Roy followed Gabi's orders. "Over, under. Over, under. Half clove hitch and—"

"Presto!" said Josh.

"Exactly," said Gabi. "Dana? Sari?"

"We're almost done," said Dana from a nearby tree.

"I need some help," said Tomer.

"Coming," said Josh.

"Now we need to gather wood to start the fire," said Gabi. "Off you go."

After what felt like forever, Josh's arms were scratched and sore from carrying branches. When everyone had finished setting wood down by the fire pit, Gabi complimented them on their teamwork.

"While we still have some light, I want to introduce you to a few ghosts," said Gabi.

"Ghosts?" said Josh. "You can't see ghosts."

"You feel them," said Tomer. "Mega-creepy."

"I heard about these ghosts who got lost in the fog," said Nate.

"What happened to them?" asked Dana.

"They were mist."

Dana groaned. "I hope they haven't found their way back here!"

"Follow me," said Gabi.

Josh and Nate stuck close together behind Gabi. Their feet crunched on the rocky ground. Prickly branches scratched at their legs. The wind played hide-and-seek, catching them unawares as they left the closed area of their zoolah and headed out through the park.

"See that tree growing inside the cistern?" asked Gabi.

"I see the tree, but what's a cistern?" asked Nate.

"It's a hole in the ground that was used to collect rain water," said Roy.

"Is there still water down there?" asked Sari.

"Let's look," said Roy, leaning over.

"Watch out for the ghosts!" said Tomer.

"Exactly," said Gabi. "That tree growing out from the middle is known as the ghost tree. Legend has it that ghosts live in the tree. In the days when the cistern was used, the kids who came to collect water were told if they hung around too long, the ghosts would come out and snatch them."

Josh gaped up at the tree. Craggy branches spread out like witches' claws from a thick trunk that disappeared deep inside the cistern. The wind had died down, and yet Josh could see the branches moving.

"That tree alone would've kept me from hanging around," Josh whispered to Nate.

"There's no such thing as ghosts," said Nate, though Josh thought he heard a quiver in his voice.

"I don't see any," said Dana.

"'Cause you can't see ghosts," said Roy. "That's why they're called ghosts."

Gabi gave a low, ominous chuckle. "Don't know if they're there now, but if the legend is true, it'll keep you guys from exploring around here without me. Now pay attention. Figure-eight stopper knots are best to use in a situation like this." Gabi tied a rope to a branch that touched the wall of the cistern and demonstrated how to pass the tail over itself to make a loop.

The Scouts watched him tighten the rope and give it a tug. "These knots don't slip; they make a strong anchor."

"True," said Sari. "But why're you making it here?"

"I'm taking you guys down to explore."

"Are you sure you want to do that?" asked Amit.

"You bet. We checked it out last week before bringing you here. There are small indentations for steps on the side of the wall. The rope's just for safety, in case you miss one. Feel around until you find a place to slip in your foot. Just be careful when you reach the bottom because if there's still water there, it can get slippery. I'll go down first. Tomer, you follow right behind me. Then Josh."

"Um, why don't I stay here and guard the rope? You know, like if anyone decides to remove it and then you guys can't get back up," said Josh.

"There's no one here but us," said Gabi. "The other Scouts are busy with their groups. The rope'll be safe. Besides, I need you all with me."

"Why?"

"You'll see. Come on."

Josh watched as first Gabi and then Tomer were swallowed up in the dark. He heard a call from somewhere down below that sounded like his name, but he wasn't sure and decided not to move.

"They're yelling at you to pull up the rope," said Roy. "Hurry. It's my turn after yours."

Josh's hands shook as he brought the rope up. He tied it around his waist as Gabi and Tomer had done, testing the knot. Kicking his foot into the side of the wall, he felt for a step. It took a few tries before Josh found the indentations.

Josh inched his way down, flattening himself to the side. "If only my palms had suction cups," he thought.

"Get a move on!" Roy shouted.

"I'm moving," said Josh. Right foot, right hand, left foot, left hand. He kept his eyes focused on the wall – he didn't look down and didn't look up. The cool damp from below drifted upwards and settled on his skin. He shivered from fear or cold, he couldn't tell which.

"Almost here," said Gabi. "The next step's a bit of a stretch, but if Tomer made it, so can you."

With the toe of his boot, Josh felt for the indentation.

"Lower," said Tomer. "A bit to the right."

Josh's right hand could barely hold on to the stone above him, but still there was no place to slip in his toe.

"A bit lower," said Gabi. "Farther right."

Josh stretched as far as his leg could go and just when he thought he'd never make it, his toe slipped inside a step. He quickly maneuvered down the rest of the way until Gabi's hand grabbed his shoulder.

"Am I safe now?" asked Josh, hesitant to move.

"You sure are," said Tomer. "The floor's rocky in places, but mostly flat."

"Nice and cool too," said Josh, taking a deep breath as he steadied himself against the wall. "Ugh! Wet goo."

"Chalk," said Gabi. "There're lots of caves in this area because the natural bedrock's soft and easy to dig through."

When they'd all made it to the bottom, Gabi had the group sit in a circle. "Look," he said, pointing at the sky.

"This hole is like a telescope," said Sari.

"I see the first stars," said Tomer.

"Too bad they're dead," said Roy.

"Roy," said Sari. "The stars are magical."

"What you see from here is how the stars looked a million years ago," said Roy. "They've been dead for ages."

"So when we stargaze," said Dana, "we don't see the present, but only the past."

"And I thought this cistern was ancient!" said Josh.

"I'm hoping to spot the constellation Orion," said Sari. "It's the perfect time of year for it."

"True," said Gabi. "Right now, though, it's time to light the Hanukkah candles. Josh?"

Josh pulled the candles from his pocket. "I thought they were for tomorrow night."

"I changed my mind 'cause I thought it'd be fun to light them down here, sing some songs and then go back to the campsite to make dinner. I'll give you more candles later."

Josh handed the Hanukkah candles to Gabi. He had to admit that it was exciting being inside the cistern, but the sounds from the ghost tree kept him from being able to really enjoy it. Was he the only one feeling this way? He sneaked a peek at the others. They looked like they were struggling to stay calm. Gabi lit the shamash and then passed it around so each Scout could light a candle.

"Now we can go, right?" asked Dana.

"Got to wait until the candles burn out," said Gabi.

"Meanwhile, I'll show you the entrance to a tunnel that leads to a burial cave."

"And the sarcophagus with the bones of the decomposed bodies," chirped Roy.

"Right," said Gabi. "There are stone steps that lead up from the cave floor to the outside ground level. It's easier to exit that way than climbing back up the cistern."

"Noooooo thanks," said Dana. "I'm climbing up the way I climbed down. This place gives me the creeps."

"Then how about a story?" said Gabi. "While we watch the candles burn."

"Or we could tell jokes," said Nate. "What did the blue candle say to the green one?"

"I don't know, Nate," said Dana. "What did the blue candle say to the green one?"

"I'm going out tonight."

Amit and Tomer, keeping the beat, slapped their left legs, then their right and gave two thumbs-up.

Josh stifled a groan, wishing Nate would quit it with the jokes. As if. He knew that when Nate was nervous, the jokes came faster.

"I know a ghost story," said Roy, "about these kids who are eaten by—"

"Thanks, Roy," said Gabi. "I've got one ready."

The story was about a rabbi who asked a young man to solve a problem about filling up a cave to win the rabbi's daughter, whom he wanted to marry. Josh was listening, but he was also watching the tree above them, which was suddenly doing things that trees were not supposed to do.

"The tree's moving!" Josh yelped.

"The ghost is coming for us!" shouted Roy.

CHAPTER 5

The tree shuddered as angry black pellets fired into the sky.

"It's alive!" Dana screamed.

Above them the ghost tree swelled and flapped its branches, morphing into a living, breathing, swooping vulture.

"Hands over your heads," yelled Amit. Josh ducked, too afraid to move, until Sari started giggling. "Birds," she said. "Of course, it's birds." Josh dared to peek skywards. "They were settling inside the tree for the night," she said, laughing. "We scared them."

"We scared them?" said Dana. "More like they scared us."

"Good thing we've got a nature expert with us," said Gabi, taking his hands off his head. "I have to admit, they got me rattled for a moment."

Josh didn't know who started giggling first, but soon they were all roaring with laughter and didn't even notice that the Hanukkah candles had burned out. It was time to head back.

The climb up the cistern was faster, and soon they were at the campsite stacking the twigs in the fire pit and getting the supplies ready to make dinner. Gabi handed Josh more candles for the following night.

"How did you figure out it was birds?" Josh asked Sari, who was building a small teepee-like structure in the fire pit and packing kindling inside it.

"I'm part of an orienteering group. We learn all sorts of amazing stuff." Sari paused to admire her work. "They taught us how to find our way without a GPS to guide us, using topographical maps and the stars. There's also a counselor called Nurit who's into plants. Nurit says she's never lonely when she goes for walks in the forest because she knows all the plants by their names so it's like she's walking with friends."

Josh laughed. "That's a bit strange."

"Is it?" Sari shrugged, then smiled. "She also told me about how birds flock together and settle in for the night around sundown. That's probably how the ghost legend started."

"By a bunch of kids like us, I bet," said Josh, handing Sari bigger sticks of wood to place on the outer side of the teepee.

Sari held the wood in her hand. "Smell that?"

"What?" said Josh. "I don't smell anything." He'd taken off his shoe to shake out a pebble. He hoped Sari wasn't talking about his feet.

"It's the carob trees," she said. "The male trees give off a powerful smell."

"Oh," said Josh, relieved.

"Their smell attracts insects that pollinate it."

Josh was still sniffing the air when Gabi came by and told them he had to join the other counselors for a quick planning session and would check in later to light the fire. Josh was so busy helping Sari that he didn't notice what the others were doing until a piercing wail shattered the silence.

"Sounds like Dana," said Sari.

"Roy threw my sleeping bag into the cistern!" Dana cried, as she ran toward them, with Roy close behind.

Roy snorted. "It was yours, Jaws? I thought it was his," he said, pointing to Josh.

"Jaws?" said Nate.

"Roy's nickname for Dana," said Tomer, "because of her braces."

They all gathered around Dana. "What am I going to do?"

"That was nasty," said Tomer.

"I guess we'd better take a look," said Sari. "Everyone get your flashlights."

They tramped back to the cistern.

"I can't even see it down there," said Dana. "How'll I get it?"

Roy shrugged. "Don't know. Not my problem."

"Yes it is," said Nate. "You threw it down there. Go get it."

"No way I'm going down there."

"Get it, Roy," Dana demanded, "or I'll find Gabi and he'll have you kicked off the trip."

"Go ahead. He won't send me home."

"Roy Bashan, if you make me cry, you're going to be sorry!" said Dana, her voice trembling.

There was an advantage to having lost their stuff after all, thought Josh. He turned to tell Nate, but his brother wasn't next to him.

"Nate?"

"Over here."

Nate was checking the knot on the rope Gabi had left tied to the ghost tree.

"What're you doing?"

"Somebody has to go down and get that bag."

"Somebody," said Josh, "doesn't mean you."

"See these mega-mosquito bites?" asked Tomer. "I got them when we were down there."

"I've got a ton too," said Josh, scratching his arm.

"Mosquitoes breed in standing water," said Sari.

"Dana, you don't need your sleeping bag," said Amit. "No one sleeps much on these campouts. Later we'll be sitting around singing and telling stories. You're making a big deal out of nothing. Gabi can get it tomorrow."

Josh peered over the edge again, teetered, and grabbed onto the rope to keep from falling.

"I do too need my sleeping bag," said Dana. "I've packed important stuff in it."

"I'll get it," said Nate.

"What're you, crazy?" said Josh. "You heard Tomer. Ghosts. Bats. Mega-mosquitoes. Have you totally lost your mind?" Josh wanted to shake him. Nate always had to play the hero, but this time he was going too far. "I'm not joking, Nate."

"I hear ya'. It's no joke," said Nate as he secured the rope around his waist and kicked off the side. "'Cause insect jokes really bug me."

There was no use arguing with Nate. Once he made up his mind, nothing could change it. Straining to see through the darkness, Josh focused on his brother's silhouette. "If anything happens to you, Mom's going to kill both of us," he shouted.

Nate didn't answer.

At least, Josh consoled himself, they'd climbed down earlier. Josh could imagine each foothold as Nate inched his way lower.

Josh clasped his hands tightly around the rope. It burned as it slid through his palms and yet the pain gave him relief, reassuring him that Nate was on the other end. Josh gauged the weight and the motion of his twin with each step. If anything happened to him… Josh forced himself to keep his thoughts focused on the rope.

"What about snakes?" asked Amit. "Don't they hunt at night?"

"Don't worry," said Roy. "The poisonous ones rattle so Nate'll be able to hear one if it comes near."

"Cut it out, Roy," said Sari. "You know there're no rattlesnakes in these parts."

Josh refused to think about snakes or spiders or mega-mosquitoes. Suddenly the rope went slack. "Nate!"

"Don't pull on it," said Tomer. "Nate might be stretching for that last step."

Earlier, when Josh had gone down, he remembered how Gabi had led them away from the damp part of the cistern to a dry ledge near the underground passage that led to the burial cave. Josh shuddered. He hoped Dana's sleeping bag had landed at the bottom of the "steps" and Nate wouldn't have to hunt around for it.

"Are you okay?" called Josh. The silence was driving him crazy.

Whoosh!

They shrieked as a swarm of beating wings rose up.

"Nate!"

No answer.

"Nate!" Josh cried.

"He's been sucked into the black hole," said Roy.

"Shut up, Roy," said Josh.

"I'm getting Gabi," said Dana.

"What's wrong, Jaws? Worried Nate won't make it, or worried about your sleeping bag?"

"Both," said Dana. She snatched the rope from Josh and held it out to Roy. "You're going down to help him."

"Wait," said Tomer. "I see a light."

"Nate's flashlight," said Amit.

Dana and Josh held the rope tightly until Nate's shadowy form appeared from the depths of the cistern, the sleeping bag strapped to his back.

"You're alive!" Josh punched him on the arm. "Am I glad those bats didn't get you. Why didn't you answer us?"

"I just wanted to get down, get the bag and get out as fast as I could."

Dana laughed. "Thanks, Nate." She untied the ropes that secured the sleeping bag to Nate's back. "Ugh! It's wet."

"It's damp down there," said Nate. "And really dark. I kept thinking about what kind of lights Noah must've used on the Ark."

"Stronger than the ones we have," said Dana.

"Yeah. I bet he used flood-lights."

They all groaned loudly as Amit and Tomer slapped, clapped and gave two thumbs-up. "You're the best, Nate! Now let's get outta here." They set off for their campsite. Sari and Dana asked Nate to help build their tent. Amit and Tomer announced they were going to search for more wood. That left Josh alone with Roy.

"Come on, Gingie. By process of elimination we've been elected to make dinner."

Josh wondered what dinner meant and if peanut butter and jelly sandwiches counted as a main course.

Roy shoved a pot into Josh's hands. "There's a tank of water over there. Fill this up."

Josh noticed the long butcher knife in Roy's hand and decided that it might not be the right time to tell Roy to stop ordering him around. Josh found his way to the water tank, stumbling over every root in his path. He was glad it was dark so he couldn't see what might be floating in the open tank. He filled the pot and staggered back, careful not to trip. In the distance he could see a small fire burning in the pit.

"Gabi was here and lit the fire, but then he had to leave again to help light other campfires. He left me in charge," said Roy.

"He did?" asked Josh.

"Yeah," said Roy. "Gabi knows my mother's boyfriend taught me about fire safety and how to keep a secure distance." Roy balanced a rack on the three sturdy rocks that surrounded a patch of burning coals. Josh thought about the propane stove he'd packed that was now in Australia. The stick fire would have to do. He set the pot on the rocks.

"When the water boils, I'll add the spaghetti. In the meantime, throw some of this tomato sauce into the pan and stir."

Josh had expected Roy to complain that cooking was girls' work, but Roy was not just opening cans, he was slicing onions, halving tomatoes, and chopping something green and bushy. Josh hoped it was edible.

"What's that?"

"They're nettles," said Sari, appearing out of nowhere. "I picked them earlier when I heard that Roy was planning to make spaghetti sauce. They add a wonderful flavor and have lots of nutrients too."

"We could use more nettles to make tea later," said Roy.

"I suppose you want me to go pick them," said Josh. "Where are they?"

Sari and Roy laughed. "Believe me," said Sari, "you don't want to pick them if you don't know how. I'll go." Sari skipped off and was swallowed up by the dark.

It was so black out, it'd be hard to tell the difference between a nettle and a patch of poison ivy, Josh thought.

"How do you know how to do all this stuff?" asked Josh as Roy chopped more of the green leaves.

"I always do the cooking on these trips. Baruch's a chef at the best hotel in Jerusalem." Roy diced the onions with electric speed. "Baruch shared some of his secrets of how to cut, slice, and chop. Decapitating lettuce heads," Roy snickered, "is my specialty."

"I bet." Josh stirred the spaghetti sauce as Roy added more vegetables. "So you live with your mom and not your dad?" he asked.

"Huh?" said Roy, keeping his eyes on the cutting board. "Yeah, I live with my mom and Baruch. My dad's dead. He was an officer in the army."

"Oh," said Josh. "I didn't know."

"See if you can find the salt," said Roy. "This is going to taste like boiled dirt if there's no salt for the water."

"Sure thing," said Josh. Taking the flashlight that Roy offered, Josh paused to glance at Roy's silhouette. He wondered what had happened to Roy's dad. He thought about how sad he'd be if anything ever happened to his own father.

CHAPTER 6

"This sauce is the best you've ever made, Roy," said Gabi, twirling the last bit of spaghetti around his fork and popping it into his mouth.

"'Cause I'm Chef Roy-al," said Roy.

Amit and Tomer slapped, clapped and gave Roy the thumbs-up.

"Nice one!" said Nate.

Sari coughed meaningfully.

"Oh, yeah," Roy said. "Josh and Sari helped too."

"Great teamwork," said Gabi. "I'm glad you remembered to mention your other helpers, Roy." He stood up. "Sorry I haven't been around much, but one of the counselors had a home emergency and just left, so we're one counselor short. I'll have to leave you alone again while I check on her campers. All the counselors are pitching in to cover for her."

"Great teamwork," said Josh.

"Exactly. Now, about the fire. Remember the rules: no getting too close to it, do not burn anything plastic, keep the flame low and in the pit. I'll be back to check on you in a while. I've laid out my sleeping bag and backpack there. You can sleep anywhere, just not too close to the fire pit." Gabi started to walk away, then turned around. "Oh, and when you've finished eating, pack up the food or you won't have anything left for tomorrow. Jackals, wild cats, and hyenas will eat whatever's around."

"Jackals, wild cats, hyenas?" said Josh.

"Jackals are afraid of people," said Sari. "And hyenas live closer to the Negev."

"Perfect," said Josh. "That leaves just the wild cats."

Once Gabi was out of earshot, Roy announced, "I cooked. It's only fair that you guys clean up."

"We're tired," said Sari. "We've lugged wood, set up tents, fetched and carried all afternoon, not to mention climbing in and out of the cistern." She rolled a stone closer to the fire and sat down. "I'm not moving."

They watched the flames jump and leap with more energy than any of them had. No one spoke. No one made a move to clear away the pile of paper plates, cups, and pots they'd used for cooking. Their packs with the food for the next day lay open on the ground.

"We can't just leave our food supplies spread around for the animals," said Nate. "Let's draw straws."

"Plastic straws are bad for the environment," said Sari.

"We could put our names in a hat," said Tomer. "Did anyone bring a pencil?"

"I've got an idea," said Roy.

Josh gulped. If it was Roy's idea, he knew he wasn't going to like it.

"Why don't we play Truth or Dare?" asked Roy. "The liars, I mean losers, have to clean up."

Dana giggled. The fire reflected off her braces. "You can tell a lot about a person by what they choose."

"Because fearless people always choose the dares," said Tomer.

"Or maybe because they're more afraid of telling the truth," said Dana. "So … who dares to play Truth or Dare?"

The last time Nate and Josh had played the game was on the Scout trip back home. Nate had accepted a dare and was half a cup away from a mouthful of worms when their Scouts guide caught and stopped him. Josh wasn't enthusiastic about telling the truth, and as for dares? Forget it!

Josh tried to catch Nate's eye, but his twin was listening to Sari as she showed him how to tie a square knot.

"These knots only work because of friction," said Sari. "If you use a nylon rope, the knot'll slide."

"How do you know all that?" Nate asked her.

"My mom sails," said Sari. "She taught me all the different knots." Sari paused. "Well—"

"Well what?" said Nate.

"I'm waiting for the wisecrack."

Nate shook his head. "No jokes. I'm too impressed. Can you show me another one?"

"Hey, you two, pay attention," said Amit. "How do we choose who goes first?"

"I'll use the shesh beish pieces," said Roy.

"I think we ate them," said Josh, who had no idea what they were, but figured it would be good news if they'd disappeared.

"Backgammon checkers," said Amit. "I guess they'll work."

Roy counted out six white checkers and one black one. "Whoever gets this white one with the black stain will ask the question. Whoever gets the black one will have to answer the question truthfully, or do the dare."

They nodded in agreement.

"One more thing," said Roy. "We keep what we're doing a secret. Nothing that happens here should leave this circle. Agreed?"

"Agreed," said everyone.

Roy dropped the backgammon checkers into a sock and held it under his nose. "Not too bad. I've only worn this one a couple of times."

"Gross," said Dana. "I'm not touching it."

"Just kidding." Roy took out a checker and passed the sock to Tomer.

Josh watched as the sock started to make the rounds.

So far, no one had picked the black piece. Now it was his turn. He took the sock from Amit. Even if he had some way to peek inside it, it was too dark to see anything. Josh stuck in his hand and pulled out a checker.

"White!" He breathed a sigh of relief.

"I got the one with the stain, so I ask," said Tomer. "Who do I ask?"

"Me," said Dana. "I picked the black one."

"Truth or dare?" asked Tomer.

Dana hesitated. "Truth."

Amit whispered something in Tomer's ear. Tomer laughed.

"What was inside your sleeping bag that made it urgent to get it tonight?"

Dana shot Sari a warning look. "Nothing," said Dana. "I just can't sleep without it. It's cold at night."

"You're lying," said Roy. "We all heard you say that you had stuff inside it. What was inside? Truth or dare."

Dana covered her face with her hands. "Squeezy," she mumbled.

"Squeezy?" said Roy. "What's a squeezy?"

"My stuffed bear. I've never spent a night without Squeezy." Dana peeked at them through her fingers. "Please swear you won't tell anyone."

"Nothing leaves this circle," said Roy.

They dumped their checkers into the bag. That wasn't so bad, thought Josh. Roy had shined his flashlight on Dana, and they'd all seen her blush, but her giggles made him think she wasn't upset. Not to mention that she didn't have to do the dishes and store the food. Squeezy had come to her rescue.

"Who's next?" asked Sari. "She held up the white checker with the stain. "It's my turn to ask." She passed the sock to Josh.

Josh reached in. "I've got the black one," he said. It fit his mood. He was worried about what would happen next.

"Truth or dare?' asked Sari. Her long honey-colored hair was pulled into a ponytail, but the light from the campfire did little to illuminate her face. Josh strained to see it more clearly. She had hazel eyes and a bunch of freckles on her nose. Josh admired the way she'd sprinted off the bus like a gazelle and dashed over the rocky terrain, calling out the name of everything green and flowering – and how she knew how to tie complicated knots, too. But now there was a tone in her voice that unnerved him in the same way that Roy could make his heart race faster than the ghost tree had.

Josh considered his options. Dare? No way, he thought. Truth?

"Well?" she said. "I'm waiting."

"Truth," said Josh finally.

"Truth." Sari laughed.

Josh dug his nails into the palm of his hand.

Sari whispered with Dana. They snickered. Josh silently counted to ten and back again, trying not to look like he had more secrets to hide than mosquito bites to scratch.

"Is it true that you and Nate bought tons of stuff for this trip? Lanterns, camp stoves, cooking gear, tents." She giggled. "And miners' hats with a light on top?"

"What if we did?" asked Nate.

"That's so—"

"Spoiled?" said Roy.

"I was going to say, so un-Scout like," said Sari. "We build things. We use nature. We don't need to buy lots of equipment to manage on our own and have a good time."

Josh wondered how Sari knew about all the stuff they'd packed. Josh shot an angry look at Amit, but Amit was looking down at his hands. He'd probably wanted to boast about all the fun equipment they had, not realizing that it would boomerang back at his cousins.

Bury me in a cave, thought Josh. True, after the first day on the trip, he'd realized that most of the stuff they'd packed wasn't necessary. This was just the ammunition Roy needed to confirm that Josh was a certified wimp.

And Roy was enjoying every moment. "Bet you can't even go for a walk unless you have some gizmo that tells you your speed."

Josh felt the heat rising from his shoes to the ends of his hair. "No!" Josh blurted out. "That's not true!"

Silence spread from one Scout to the other.

"You're lying," said Sari finally.

"It's the truth," said Josh. "You asked if we bought all the equipment that got re-routed to Australia. Technically, we didn't buy any of it. Our parents did!"

"That's not what I meant," said Sari.

"Too bad," said Josh, breathing a sigh of relief. "That's what you asked. I answered you. I told the truth. No dish duty for me! Pass the sock so we can have another round."

"My turn!" said Tomer. "I got the black one. Who's asking?"

"Me," said Dana. "Truth or dare?"

"Dare!"

Dana and Sari huddled together again. "You know how Gabi bossed us around all day? Lash this, watch the fire, put away the stuff?" said Dana.

"Yeah," said Tomer.

"We think it's time to have a bit of fun with Gabi."

"Where do I come in?" asked Tomer.

"See that tree?"

They all looked at the tree with the thick trunk and rough scratchy branches.

"That oak tree?" asked Tomer.

Sari nodded. "Exactly. See where Gabi tossed his stuff? We want you to climb the tree and stick a pail of water in the nook between the two branches."

Dana continued. "Camouflage the pail with leaves and stuff so we can't see it. Attach a rope to Gabi's hat and hang it from one of the branches securing the pail. Make it appear like all we've done is string up his hat. He'll think it's a cute prank."

"Except when Gabi pulls the string, he'll get—"

"A cold shower!" said Roy. "I love it!"

Tomer shimmied up the tree. Nate filled the pail with water and they made a pulley to lift it. After a few tries, Tomer figured out how to balance the bucket so that one tug on the rope would overturn it.

"Let me test it," said Roy. "I'm fast and can jump out

of the way before the water hits me." He took off his shirt just in case.

"Ready?" said Tomer

Everyone held their breaths.

Roy tugged at the rope that was attached to Gabi's hat.

Nothing happened.

"It's not working," said Roy. He looked up the tree at Tomer, who at that moment released the pail, and SPLASH! Roy got a face full of water.

"Hey!"

"It works!" said Josh. "Way to go, Tomer."

"Not funny," Roy sputtered, laughing.

Once they rigged up the pail again and Roy had changed into dry clothes, it was time to pass the sock around. Roy picked the stained checker and Nate got the black one.

Josh held his breath, waiting to see what Nate would do—tell the truth or accept a dare? He had that knotty feeling in his stomach again.

CHAPTER 7

Nate cleared his throat. "So what'll it be, Roy?"

Roy poked at the fire, the embers casting an eerie glow on his face. "You tell me. Truth? Dare? Double dare?"

Say "truth," Josh wanted to tell Nate. No matter how you answer, I'll cover for you. Josh watched the staring contest between Roy and Nate with a sinking feeling. He knew Nate couldn't resist a challenge.

Nate crossed his arms and sat up straighter. "Dare," he said.

Typical, thought Josh. Why can't Nate be sensible for once? A silent hush fell over the group. A log on the fire split apart, sending sizzling sparks into the air. I've got to stop him, thought Josh, before Roy dares him to do something he'll regret later.

"Let's forget it," said Josh. "I'll clean."

"No," said Nate. "I'm not afraid of anything you can think up, Roy. I'll even do a double dare."

"Nate!" Josh yelped.

For a moment even Roy seemed taken aback. But then he said, "Remember the cistern?"

"What about it?" asked Nate.

"Remember how Gabi pointed out the underground

passage that leads to the burial cave with the sarcophagus?"

"The box of bones?" said Nate.

"Yeah," said Roy. "I crawled through it with Baruch. Once you get to the cave, there're stairs that lead out. I dare you to do the same thing—go down into the cistern, crawl through the tunnel into the burial cave and climb out by the steps to where we'll be waiting for you."

"Roy," said Amit. "That's not a double dare, that's a quadruple dare!"

"If it were easy," said Roy, "we wouldn't call it a dare."

Nate froze as if turned to stone.

"Well?" said Roy.

"I've already been inside the cistern on my own," said Nate.

"But not through the cave," said Roy.

"I know."

Josh noticed a muscle twitching above his brother's jaw.

"I'll do it," said Nate.

"If you don't make it through," said Roy, "we'll know you chickened out and you'll have to clean up the mess here."

Nate's lips were set in a stubborn line. "No prob,"

he said. "Roll up your sleeves, Roy. Your elbows will be deep in soapy water soon." Josh saw that Nate's muscle was no longer twitching. It would be impossible to stop him now.

"We'll see," said Roy. "It'll be a miracle if you actually make it through to the end. Imagine crawling through a narrow tunnel in absolute darkness, underneath the ground – like a vampire."

Josh gulped. "Nate should at least have a flashlight," he protested. "The Jews had torches with them when they were fighting the Romans in these tunnels."

Sari, Amit and Tomer nodded in agreement. "At least a flashlight," Amit echoed. "That is if you even agree to do it. You don't have to, you know."

"I'm not scared," said Nate, but Josh heard a slight quiver in his brother's voice. Climbing down into a hole to get Dana's sleeping bag was easy for Nate, who wasn't afraid of heights. Cramped spaces were a different story. Although Nate was usually the braver twin, narrow, dark places terrified him.

When they'd lived in their old house in Queens, they'd had a chute that cannoned straight into the laundry room in the basement. Josh had dared Nate to slide down the chute. If it had worked, it would have been a great escape route if they ever needed one. But it hadn't worked. Nate got stuck in the chute until their mom came home from work and called their dad, who tugged him out. Feeling the walls close in around him had made it hard for Nate to breathe, and he almost passed out. Their parents grounded both boys for a week, and Nate had been afraid of enclosed spaces ever since. What if Nate froze and got stuck in the middle of the tunnel?

"Take my flashlight," said Amit.

Josh took Nate's arm and let the others go ahead as they left the campfire.

Nate stopped and set Amit's flashlight on the ground while he bent down to tie his shoelaces. Josh nudged his brother away and picked up the torch before Nate could retrieve it.

"Let me be the one to go down there," whispered Josh.

"I can't let you do that," said Nate. "I got myself into this."

"And I convinced you to go into the laundry chute, remember? Consider us even."

"Hey, you two," called Roy. "Hurry!"

"What if they find out?" asked Nate.

"They won't," said Josh. "We'll only tell them after Roy has cleaned up. Show them that we can outsmart Roy."

Nate draped his arm around his brother's shoulder. "You're sure you can do this?"

Josh nodded. He didn't trust his voice.

"Way to go, Josh," said Nate. "You're as brave as a skeleton."

"What's that supposed to mean?" asked Josh.

"The skeleton had nobody to go with him either."

"Nate," Josh hissed. "No joking. You'll give us away."

When they joined the others, Josh pushed his hair over his birthmark.

They all stopped to stare at the ghost tree.

"Let me check the rope," said Sari.

"Oh, and Nate," said Roy. "Stay to the right. That's what Baruch told us to do when we crawled through."

Stay to the right, Josh repeated in his head.

"Are you sure we should let him do this?" asked Dana. "Gabi will be really mad if he finds out, and he'll be here any minute to check on us."

"Everything that goes on in this circle stays in the circle. Gabi won't find out. Not unless someone tells him, or he shows up in the next half hour, which is unlikely. Besides, it was Gabi who told us about the tunnel in the first place," said Roy.

"This whole thing is making me very uncomfortable," said Dana. "Don't do it, Nate."

Josh shook his head. He was getting more nervous by the second, but he had to do this. Not only would he be helping Nate, but if he succeeded, he'd prove that he could be braver than his twin – braver than all of them.

"It's getting late," said Roy. "Hear those jackals? They'll be eating our breakfast if you don't get a move on. And besides, we have to get back to the campsite before Gabi does."

"Let's get this over with," said Tomer. "It's okay, Nate, we'll be waiting for you by the cave's exit."

Josh exhaled. He gave a tug on the rope as Nate held it securely in his hands. He turned to look one last time at the shadowy figures standing by the side of the cistern. Trying not to think about the dangers below, Josh slid over the side and plunged into the darkness.

CHAPTER 8

Feeling for the footholds, Josh edged himself into the cistern. The air was clammy and smelled like stinky feet. Josh steadied himself against the wall, slime coating his hands.

"Chalk," he said, reminding himself of Gabi's explanation.

Josh was sure he'd be paralyzed with fear once his feet touched the ground. But, to his amazement, when he got to the bottom and looked up, he saw the sky was covered by a myriad of stars, and somehow he wasn't as frightened as he'd expected.

"Made it!" he shouted, waving his flashlight.

Josh didn't care what Roy said about the stars. He loved the way they sparkled, formed patterns, and lit up the heavens as if millions of Hanukkah candles were shining in every part of the world at exactly the same moment. A pigeon cooed. Josh remembered that hidden somewhere in the branches of the ghost tree were bird nests.

As Josh was taking stock of his surroundings, his flashlight flickered and went out. Josh whacked it against his thigh. It came on again, revealing the gaping black hole that Gabi had said was the entrance to the underground passage.

"Nate?" shouted Dana. "Are you okay?"

"I'm fine," yelled Josh. He whacked the flashlight again. The battery had better not give out. Taking a deep breath, Josh crouched down and rested his knees against the entrance. He pointed the beam inside.

Crawling while holding the flashlight was going to be awkward. If only he had his miner's hat with the light on the cap. He slid his right hand forward and followed it with his right knee. He repeated the same motion with his left. Like a toddler, Josh crept forward on all fours, keeping his head down and away from the low ceiling. Things were going okay – until the flashlight spluttered and went out. Josh shook it. He tapped it against the wall. He begged it to turn on. Nothing. Just darkness.

Something tickled the scruff of his neck. Josh screeched and pulled his sweater over his head. Clamping his lips together to keep his teeth from chattering, he coaxed himself to move on.

He shoved the useless flashlight into his pocket and crawled forward. "Stay calm," he told himself. Despite the dampness in the tunnel, Josh felt a drop of sweat slide down the side of his face. Sweat? No, a tear, he realized, tasting the salty drop on his tongue. This was crazy! What was he doing? How had he let himself get into this mess? Another tear trickled down his cheek. He brushed it away. He'd be stuck in the cave forever if he didn't keep moving.

The farther Josh crawled, the more he hated himself for taking Nate's place. He hated Nate for choosing a dare. He hated Roy. He hated his cousin Amit for giving him a broken flashlight when he had a brand new one in Australia. So what if he wriggled out bottom first? He'd find Gabi and ask him to call Aunt Tamar to take him back to Jerusalem. He was done with trying to be a Scout.

As Josh started reversing, something in his shirt pocket brushed against his chest: the Hanukkah candles that Gabi had given him for the next night. In ancient times, didn't they light the way? Wasn't that the whole point of the Hanukkah holiday? The Maccabees were outnumbered. There wasn't enough oil to burn and provide light for one night, and yet it lasted for eight days. Not only that, the small band of Maccabees defeated their enemies and secured the Temple in Jerusalem. To Josh, his situation seemed as dark as it had been for the Jews back then. As with the Maccabees, a little light would give him hope and the strength to go on.

With shaking fingers, Josh dug into his pocket and pulled out a candle, then found the matches in his other pocket.

"Let there be light!" he said aloud, and, laughing

to himself, he continued to crawl backwards. Soon, though, he realized that the candle wouldn't help him to see behind him, only what loomed ahead, and turning around was not an option because the tunnel was too narrow. Besides, with light, the tunnel seemed less scary. It would be easier to go on.

Josh made a tight fist and wedged the candle into the crook of his hand. Slowly, so as not to blow out the flame or burn himself with wax, he inched ahead.

"Keep to the right," Roy had said. Josh wanted to trust that Roy knew what he was talking about.

With his shoulder grazing the wall, Josh kept a steady pace, trying to ignore his clammy palms and the pain in his knees as he dragged himself across the uneven rocks scratching through his uniform. He tried to convince himself that the acrid smell had nothing to do with the old bones waiting for him in the burial cave.

"Or headless skeletons," Josh said aloud, remembering Roy's description of the decapitated bodies. How much more of this? he wondered.

He came to a stop. There were three forks!

Roy had said there were only two.

"Now what?" said Josh, as panic rose in his throat.

The flame flickered. Josh stuck his head into the left-hand tunnel. His hand slipped and the candle flew from his grasp. It spun through the air and snuffed out. Josh screamed! Flattening himself onto his belly, he slithered backwards. Seconds later he heard the faint sound of the candle hitting a rock below. If he'd moved ahead another inch it could have been him. He had been centimeters away from falling into a hole!

He chomped down hard on his lip, tried to sit up, and bashed his head on the low ceiling. His knees were aching to stretch. The palms of his hands were raw and sore. But nothing, nothing was worse than the darkness.

Josh slipped another candle from his pocket and lit it. In the tunnel farthest to his right, a rush of fresh air blew toward him. The flame flickered. Cupping his hand around it, Josh waited until the light grew strong again. That must be the way to go. He started crawling, feeling the tunnel descend. He had to be close to the end. All that remained was the cave with the decomposed bodies—he gulped—and finally the stairs and exit. Soon he'd be above ground! He moved forward as fast as he could.

Emerging from the tunnel, Josh stood up. He'd made it into the cave! It felt great to stretch his legs. The stairs were just a few feet away. Then he froze. Right in front of him was the sarcophagus, blocking his way. The stone coffin lay smack in the middle of the cave. He had to pass right by it to reach the stairs.

Josh swallowed. "No ghosts inside there," he said. Just bones."

Josh inhaled deeply and tried to exhale his fear. The candle flame went out, but light came from above. It had to be from the Scouts' flashlights at the top of the stairs. Throwing the candle aside, Josh ran.

"I see him," said Nate. "He's at the bottom of the stairs!"

What a relief to hear Nate's voice, thought Josh, as he scrambled up the last few steps.

"He's here," said Nate. "Three cheers! But everybody, we better keep our distance when he comes out."

"Why?" asked Dana, shining her flashlight on Josh, who was panting heavily.

"Bat breath!" Nate laughed at his own joke. The others looked from Nate to Josh. Josh groaned. Only his brother would make a joke like that.

"Double cross!" shouted Roy, pointing his finger. "That's not Nate, that's Josh."

They had been found out.

CHAPTER 9

Josh stood on shaky legs. His pants were covered with chalk and his fingers with dirt. He'd imagined that everybody would greet him with slaps on the back and cheers, but now that they knew that he and Nate had switched places, Josh wasn't sure what would happen.

It wasn't fair. None of them would have taken the dare. None of them would have crawled through the tunnel in pitch darkness.

"We were going to tell you," Nate said.

"After you made me do all the work," said Roy.

"I knew it," said Amit.

"You did?" said Tomer.

"Well, sort of."

"My cousins pulled tricks on us all the time," said Dana. "You almost fooled us."

"Until Nate had to crack a joke." Josh grumbled.

"Sorry," said Nate, shuffling his feet in the dirt.

"It was Nate's dare and he chickened out," said Roy. "That means Nate has to clean up."

Nate sighed. "I know."

"Actually it was my idea for us to change places," Josh said. "Come on, Nate. I'll help you."

"Teamwork," said Nate, putting his arm around Josh.

"Josh was brave to go through the tunnel," said Sari.

"He did the dare. It doesn't seem right that he should also have to clean."

"But he and Nate cheated," said Roy.

"It's just a stupid game," said Dana. "Sari's right. We should all help. And we'd better get going before Gabi sees that the mess is still there."

"Not me. I cooked," said Roy.

"I'm too tired to fight with you," said Dana. She turned toward the campsite, her flashlight leading the way as the others followed.

"What was it like down there?" Dana asked Josh.

"Dark, stinky and scary."

Dana laughed. "I bet! That sure was a kind thing you did for your brother."

Josh hesitated. "Kind? How about brave and daring?"

"That, too," said Dana. "But I saw Nate's first reaction when Roy told him the dare. He was terrified. You jumped in like a good brother should." She sighed. "I . . . " she said, and stopped. "Never mind."

"What?"

"I hope I'll be loyal like you when my new baby brother or sister's born. My mom's going to have a baby."

Josh wanted to say that siblings were always there for each other and it was no big deal, but Dana made him feel that it was a big deal. Suddenly "kind" felt better than brave and daring.

They walked in silence.

"What was that?" said Dana, hesitating as a shrill cry pierced the darkness.

"Sounds like someone's being strangled," said Nate.

"Jackals," said Tomer.

"Jackals?" asked Josh. "Where?"

"Close by," said Tomer.

"Are they dangerous?" asked Josh.

"Jackals love raw meat," said Roy. "They watch the sky, and when they see a vulture swoop down to feast on the dead carcass below, they race ahead to get there first. After a jackal has finished devouring the remains of an animal, there isn't one bone left to lick."

Josh's tongue stuck to his throat. He wondered if the jackals knew the difference between human bones and animal bones.

"They also eat fruit," said Sari.

"A balanced diet," said Nate. "How healthy."

"They only eat fruit if there's nothing better around," said Roy.

Another cry sounded. It seemed even closer.

"I don't see our fire ahead," said Dana. "Are you sure we're going the right way?"

"Must have burned down low," said Roy. "We should've left someone behind to feed it."

"Dana, stop!" shouted Sari.

Dana froze. "What is it?" She lifted her flashlight and yelped.

Two pairs of laser eyes stared back at them. "Help!" she squealed.

"Shuffle and stamp," ordered Sari.

"Shuffle?" Josh had no idea what Sari was talking about. He was ready to turn and run. But Sari shone the flashlight on the jackals and started jumping up and down. She screamed as if she'd been bitten by a dog.

"Come on everyone, yell!" she shouted. Josh joined the others as they cried, screamed and bellowed, stomping their feet and hollering as loud as they could like wild animals about to attack.

A few moments later, panting and breathless, Sari swung her flashlight around their campground. The jackals were gone.

"We did it," said Nate. "We frightened them away."

"That was quick thinking, Sari," said Amit.

Dana groaned. "All our hot dogs are gone." She kicked a bag and out spilled a few apples with bite marks in them. "Gross," she said. "I'm not touching anything here. It's probably all infected with rabies."

The campsite looked like a cyclone had swept through it, upturning, trampling and tearing through everything.

"At least we don't have to put away the food," said Nate. "The jackals did the job for us."

They all groaned.

"We'd better throw out what they left behind, or more wild animals will show up," said Sari, handing out garbage bags.

"What happened here?" asked Gabi, running into the campsite. "I heard screaming. Is everyone okay?"

"Jackals," said Sari.

"I told you—"

"To put away our stuff, we know," said Amit.

"So what happened? Where were you?"

"Josh thought he heard something, so we went to check it out," said Roy.

"And?" asked Gabi, looking at Josh. One thing Josh was sure of, he didn't want to tell Gabi what he and Nate had done. He knew it was against the rules.

"It turned out to be nothing," Josh muttered. "Just my imagination."

Gabi nodded. "The night can play tricks on you," he said.

"So can twins," said Roy under his breath.

Josh was relieved that Gabi didn't seem to have heard that.

"Let's pack what's left of the food in bags and hang them in a tree, or tomorrow we're going to be very hungry," said Gabi.

"Tomer's great at hanging stuff in trees," said Roy with a straight face, while everyone tried not to laugh.

After securing the bags where animals couldn't get to the leftovers, the Scouts gathered around the campfire. Roy blew on the coals until the fire came back to life. Josh warmed his hands and tried to get the chill out of his body. He was exhausted. With no tent to crawl into, he spread out his sheet and rolled himself up inside it.

Somewhere far away a jackal's mournful cry was answered by another call.

"Get some sleep, Scouts," said Gabi. "Tomorrow is a big day. We've got a lot planned."

Josh shut his eyes, hoping sleep would come quickly. But his thoughts, like the hungry jackals, picked through everything that had happened to him in the last twenty-four hours.

CHAPTER 10

Josh yawned and rubbed his eyes. They were caked with grit. He had dirt up his nose. He had enough dirt in his ears for plants to start growing. His hands looked like they'd been cast in clay. He was glad he couldn't see his face. He didn't need a shower. He needed to run through a car wash. His stomach grumbled.

"Hey, sleepyhead," said Sari. "Are you hungry?"

Josh groaned. "Don't remind me. My stomach feels like the inside of the cave: hollow, cold and black."

Sari laughed. "Here's a bottle of water. After you rinse off, you can help me make breakfast."

Josh wormed out from under his sheet and tossed it aside. He wanted to ask Sari what was left for breakfast after the jackals' visit.

He washed off a layer of soot and went to find himself a tree.

At the campsite, he found Sari poking at the coals in the fire pit.

"Hey, Sari-ella, what're you searching for?"

"Potatoes. Last night Roy tossed a bunch of potatoes into the fire before we left for the cistern. In all the excitement we forgot to eat them. With a sprinkle of roasted herbs on top, they'll make a great breakfast."

Josh rolled a big stone over to the fire and sat down. He picked up a stick and jostled the coals, looking for hidden potatoes.

"It's hard to tell the difference between the potatoes and the coal."

"You'll figure it out," said Sari. "Meanwhile, I'll make some tea."

"There is no tea," said Josh. "The jackals ripped open the plastic bag with the tea bags and scattered the sugar and tea everywhere. We had to toss it all."

"I wouldn't have drunk that poison anyway. You keep fishing for those potatoes while I make the best cup of tea you'll ever taste."

Josh watched Sari skip off, hopping from plant to plant, sniffing, picking, and pocketing before moving to another bush.

Nate tossed off his sheet and sat up. "Hungry," he mumbled.

Josh kept digging around in the coals. If he were at home now he'd be eating lightly buttered toast with jam and an egg, sunny side up, and drinking a glass of chocolate milk. He sighed, rolled out a black charcoal blob, and set it on a stone. He brushed off the soot, sliced it in half, and saw that the inside was white, steamy and soft. He took a bite. It wasn't a typical breakfast, but it wasn't half bad either. Once he'd found all the potatoes, he tossed a handful of kindling on the fire and fanned it until the flames grew stronger.

"Put olive oil in the pan," said Sari. "Heat it up and then add this to the potatoes." She handed him a stick that had small leaves and a few thorns on it.

"What is it?"

"Azov, or maybe you call it zatar."

Josh frowned at the spiky twig. "I think we'd call it a weed and throw it away."

"It's not a weed." She rolled her eyes. "It's a shrub that grows wild around here. Most people grind it up and mix it with salt to sprinkle on their pita bread. I even managed to find some herbs for tea."

"Great," said Josh, who had no idea what she was talking about. Even so, she sounded so enthusiastic he didn't want to disappoint her. He tossed a log on the fire.

The aroma of the spices soon spread through the campsite. Amit and Tomer got up.

"Something smells yummy," said Amit.

"Come and get it while it's hot," said Josh.

"We're coming," said Amit. "We need to wash first."

Sari held a cup of tea under Josh's nose.

"I made this for you," she said.

"Thanks." Josh grimaced at the pee-colored water with stuff floating inside it. "Isn't that a – leaf?"

Sari flicked out the floating bit with her finger. "Taste it. I promise it won't kill you."

"You're sure?"

"Scout's honor."

Josh bent his head over the steaming liquid. It smelled okay. But how would it taste? He was thinking of telling Sari he was allergic—but allergic to what? He had no idea what she'd added.

"I'll wait till it cools off," he said.

"It tastes best hot," said Sari

Josh took a sip, expecting to gag, choke, and keel over dead. But the hot tea tasted kind of sweetish and felt good in his empty stomach.

"Not bad," he said. He took a longer drink.

"I knew you'd like it," said Sari.

Roy wandered over to the fire. His electrified hair was more matted than the thorny zatar bush. His eyes were swollen and ringed with soot. His shirt was stained black and tomato-sauce red. He ran his hand through his hair. "Smells like zatar," he said.

Sari smiled. "Josh made us breakfast while you sloths were sleeping. We watched the sun rise, too."

Josh thought about how the sun had crept up into

the sky like a flower in slow motion, blossoming into pink, orange and yellow rays.

Tomer took a bite of a baked potato. "Yum," he said. "After last night, I'm starving."

They were sitting around the small fire when they heard a shout.

"ARGHHHHH!"

The Scouts burst out laughing.

"Who?!" shouted Gabi. "What?! You guys are going to get it!"

With wet hair plastered to his face and water dripping from every part of him, Gabi stomped angrily toward the fire pit. "Which one of you—"

The Scouts looked at him innocently.

"Hungry?" said Nate, offering him a potato.

"Good shower?" asked Sari.

Dana handed him a towel. Gabi sat down by the fire and threw the towel over his shoulder. He took a potato. "You got me," he said, "but don't try anything else again, or . . . well, I might not be so forgiving."

Gabi shook out his curls, spraying the Scouts with water. After he wolfed down the potato, he said, "While I dry off and get dressed, you guys need to pack. We'll be on our way within the hour."

"Pack?" Dana moaned. "It took us hours to unpack and set up camp."

"Where's your spirit, Dana? We're Scouts. I don't want to hear any complaining."

"But, Gabi," Amit objected.

"The only 'butts' around here are the kind that have to get moving. Chop! Chop!"

Josh looked around the campsite. Funny how after only a few hours a place could feel like home. He didn't feel like leaving either. He wanted more tea. He'd been hoping to spend some time with Tomer, who had promised to show him a few of his climbing tricks.

"At least taking things down is a lot faster than putting them up," said Sari.

Exhausted from the previous night, they moved around clumsily like bats in the daytime, bumping into each other as they unhitched, unlashed, rolled up, boxed in, patted down, and threw out until there was nothing left but the smoldering embers of the fire. Gabi shoveled dirt on the coals to bury them.

"Great job, Scouts," said Gabi. "Ready to board the bus for our next stop?"

"Sure," said Amit. "We're coming."

As they grabbed their bags and started walking toward the bus, Gabi pulled them aside and said, "I didn't want to spoil breakfast, but now I have something serious to discuss with you."

"It was just a fun prank," said Roy.

"The water, yes. But one of the other counselors overheard some of you talking about what else you guys did last night."

Josh grew very still.

Gabi looked from one Scout to the other. "I should punish all of you for being so irresponsible."

Was this it, wondered Josh. Now that he wanted to stay, was Gabi going to throw him off the trip? Josh waited to hear what the others would say.

"Only Josh crawled inside," said Roy. "The rest of us watched to make sure nothing happened to him. We were very responsible."

"That's lame, Roy," said Gabi. "You all should've known better. You need to learn that actions have consequences."

"We're sorry," said Dana. "It was foolish. Josh isn't the only one to blame." Dana looked straight at Roy. "We were all involved."

"So what're you going to do about it?" asked Roy.

"I'm not sure yet," said Gabi.

Josh caught the look that Gabi gave him and turned away. He knew he was going to be the one who'd have to pay.

CHAPTER 11

Josh was the last to board the bus. He stood at the front, not sure where to sit. Dana had plunked down beside Nate. She started to get up, but Josh shook his head. He didn't feel like sitting with any of them, even Nate, knowing that he was responsible for getting them all in trouble. If only he'd stopped the game and convinced the others that the dare was reckless instead of going along with it and changing places with his twin.

Josh plopped himself next to Matt, who was sitting in the first seat behind the driver. His hair had a few twigs in it, the only sign that he'd spent the night in the woods.

"How's it going?" asked Matt.

Josh shrugged. "Okay, I guess. Where've you been? I haven't seen you around."

"I've been around, but you've been too busy to notice. I may be quiet, but I observe everything that's going on."

Josh sneaked a sideways glance at Matt. Did he know about what had happened in the cistern?

"Isn't it kind of weird being on your own when everyone else is with a group?" asked Josh.

Matt laughed. "That's the trick: being on your own when you're part of a crowd."

Josh stared out the window at the scenery speeding by. The little towns and communities were playing a game of hide and seek with the landscape. There were stretches of brown fields with nothing to see, but when the bus turned a corner, a whole bunch of roofs and boxy houses popped up. Josh wondered what it would be like to live in the middle of nowhere. Wouldn't he miss going to the mall? What if he wanted to see a movie? How big was the school around here? Did people know the names of their neighbors? And what if one of your neighbors was like Roy? Josh turned to Matt.

"You know what happened, don't you?" said Josh.

"I know that you're sitting with me instead of with your buddies. You must be feeling bad about something. Or maybe you need time by yourself to get your thoughts together."

"Maybe," said Josh. "Or maybe I wish I could turn back time."

"Well, you can't," said Matt.

The bus lurched to a stop.

"Listen up, Scouts," said Gabi. "We're making a short stop here to visit the Cave of the Twins."

"Nate and Josh's first home?" asked Roy.

"Good one," said Gabi. "But, no. It's also called the Bat Cave."

"Bats are amazing," said Tomer. "They have super-sonic hearing."

"Who do they need to talk to?" asked Dana.

"Each other," said Tomer. "They screech and chirp a lot."

"You know what's more amazing than a talking bat?" said Nate. "A spelling bee!"

"That's enough, Nate. Off the bus, everyone!" said Gabi. "It's a bit of an uphill hike to get to the cave, but once you're there, you won't be disappointed. I promise you've never heard or seen anything like it. Keep to the trails. Watch out for the wild foxes and rodents, and maybe you'll even spot a gazelle. We'll have a light snack here, and then lunch in the caves at Beit Govrin, where we'll spend our last night. Take your packs. The bus has to collect the other Scout groups that will be hiking near here."

"What about me, Gabi?" asked Josh, after everyone had gotten off the bus.

"You'll come with us, but you can't go into the cave. You've done enough cave exploration already. You'll have to wait outside until we're done. You can guard the packs, so the animals won't steal them while we're inside."

"Why only me?" said Josh. "We were all in on it."

"True," said Gabi. "But you should've known better than to follow through with the dare. This way, you'll feel bad being left behind, and your friends will feel bad leaving you behind."

"I'll stay with you," said Nate.

"Me too!" said Dana.

Josh shook his head. "No reason why you guys have to suffer. Besides, if you join the others, you can tell me what's inside."

"I'll bring up the rear," said Sari, as they started to climb the hill.

"Good thinking," said Gabi.

Sari pointed to a piece of broken brown clay by her foot.

"A pottery shard," she said, handing it to Josh. "Rub your finger over it."

Josh took it from her. "Smooth."

"It's probably a few thousand years old," said Sari. "The ancient people who lived here made clay pots to hold their food. I bet if we dug around some more, we'd find bones, fossils and teeth."

"Gross," said Dana. "Teeth! Who wants to find a bunch of teeth?"

"A paleontologist would," said Tomer, who'd slowed down to join them.

Josh whistled. "Wow, I've never touched anything so old. Can I have it?" he asked.

"No," said Sari. "We should put it back."

Tomer took the piece from Josh and held it in his palm. "As Scouts, we're taught that the less we interfere with the land, the more will be left for others to enjoy."

Sari nodded. "He's right. And this way, archeologists can study these remains to piece together our history."

Tomer carefully returned the shard to where Sari had found it.

It was a tough climb. The Scouts made their way up a steep mountain slope, walking through a dry waterbed littered with rocks and stones. A few times Josh almost lost his balance. Once he went tumbling backwards.

"Are you okay?" asked Sari.

"Sure," said Josh. "These rocks have chicken pox." He showed the rock to Sari. Though smooth, it had a bunch of holes in it.

Sari took the rock and examined it. "Caustic rock," she said. "It's what all these rocks are made from. That's why there are so many caves in this area. The ground is soft, and any pressure, like the rains which caused these indentations, creates holes."

Josh set the rock down and concentrated on ducking

branches and finding secure places to step. Sari was like a goat. Hopping from one stone to another, she barely paused to see where she'd landed.

"Most of the caves were discovered by accident," said Sari. "I visited this place with my orientation group. Beit Govrin, where we're going next, and other similar caves were man-made."

"So some caves were manmade and others were caused by natural conditions, like the hole I almost stumbled into last night?" asked Josh.

Sari laughed. "You got it. Part planning, part serendipity."

"Serendipity," repeated Josh, wondering, if given the chance, he could stumble onto some great discovery that might redeem him in Gabi's eyes. They arrived at a clearing, and all the Scouts gathered together.

"Drop your gear here," said Gabi.

The Scouts piled their backpacks under a tree.

"Josh will stay behind. We'll be about an hour. If any animals come along, Josh, remember to stamp your feet and make some noise, and they'll run off, just like last night."

"What about Matt?" asked Josh. "Can't he stay with me?"

"I'll double back to make sure you're okay, but I

have to stick with the others. You'll be fine. It's safe and, besides, we won't be that long." said Matt.

"Sure," Josh said, but he couldn't help wondering what Gabi would have done with the packs if he hadn't been there to watch them and guard the food.

The others hiked up to the cave's entrance.

"Make sure you keep your voices down," Josh heard Gabi say. "No matches or candles. Use your flashlights, but don't blind the bats, since they're hibernating. If we're quiet, we won't wake them."

"Yuck," said Dana.

"Shhhh," said Gabi.

After everyone had gone into the cave, Josh snuck up to the entrance and peered inside. It was pitch black. Just then, a piercing scream came from out of the darkness.

"Something touched me!" he heard Dana shriek.

"Calm down, Dana, bats are good. Follow me and stay close. Remember, don't shine your light directly on them. We don't want to disturb them," said Gabi.

"The last thing I want to do is disturb them," wailed Dana.

Josh walked back to the tree where the bags were stacked. He didn't want Gabi to catch him snooping around by the cave entrance. And he didn't want anything to happen to the gear either.

He lay down, leaning his head on the packs. Even though he was disappointed that he couldn't explore the cave, he was also glad to have some time to himself. Rays of sunlight slipped through the trees, warming his face. A few clouds drifted lazily above him. It was peaceful: just Josh, the trees, the clouds and the occasional twitter of a bird.

Josh felt his eyelids become heavy. He yawned and let his head fall sideways, his breath slowing as he began to drift off. Pushing a backpack aside, he rolled onto his stomach and rested his head on a grassy patch of earth.

Suddenly Josh heard a strange sound. His eyes opened wide.

"That's weird," he said aloud.

It sounded like someone was calling from beneath the ground. He sat up. The noise stopped.

I must have imagined it, he thought. Thinking about ghosts, bones, and sarcophagi was making him edgy. Josh lay down and closed his eyes again. He told himself he was having a delayed reaction to creeping through the burial cave the night before.

"Help!" the voice called.

Josh jumped up. "Stop messing with me," he cried. "I don't believe in ghosts." He put his head back down, this time a bit farther from where he'd heard the voice, and stuck his fingers in his ears. "Finally," he said. "I can get some sleep."

After a few moments, he pulled a finger from one ear.

"Help! Help me!"

Josh had no choice. He had to check it out.

The sound was coming from behind a prickly bush. He parted the branches and peeked through the tangled shrub. He heard weeping. Peering over the rim, he looked down into a gaping hole.

"Hello?" he called.

"Help!"

"Who's—who's there?"

"Josh!" The voice shouted. "Get me out of here."

It was Sari!

CHAPTER 12

"Sari? Is that really you?"

"Yes! I'm stuck."

Josh squinted into the dark again. He couldn't see a thing.

"It's really creepy in here," said Sari. "Get me out!"

"Hang on. I'll go call Gabi."

"No! Don't leave me in the dark."

"Turn on your flashlight."

"I dropped it when I fell and now I can't find it. Can I have yours?"

"The batteries are dead."

"And everyone else took their flashlights into the cave," said Sari.

"Don't panic. I have an idea," said Josh. He had used the matches Gabi had given him the night before, but he had seen Matt stick another box inside his backpack. "I'll be fast."

Quickly Josh located Matt's bag and found the matchbox. Pulling off his sweater, Josh tied one of the sleeves into a knot, tucked the pack of matches inside it, and fastened the other sleeve to a stick.

"Sari? Are you okay?" he said when he got back. "I

found some matches. I'll lower them down inside the sleeve of my sweater. If you're cold, you can put on the sweater, too."

"Thanks," she said. "I'm glad you're here, Josh."

Josh thought about running to the mouth of the cave and yelling inside for Gabi, but Gabi said noise would wake up the bats, which might make things worse for everyone.

"Ouch!" Sari shouted. "I burned my finger." The light inside flickered for an instant and went out.

"Wait a second. I'll be right back."

Josh took out another one of the Hanukkah candles. He searched around until he found a perfectly pock-sized rock. The holes seemed to be the right size for the bottom of the candle. He put the candle and the rock inside Nate's sweater and carefully lowered them down.

"Light the candle, Sari, and stick the candle inside one of the holes in the rock. That way the wax won't drip on you."

A few minutes later, a small halo of light appeared around Sari.

"Good thinking," she said. "I'm not afraid of jackals or birds, but being alone in here is really scary."

Josh peered down. He remembered how frightened he'd been the night before. In the candlelight, he saw that the hole wasn't very deep, although Sari was just far enough down to be out of reach.

"What happened?" asked Josh.

"I was walking behind everyone, when I noticed an interesting indentation in the wall of the cave. I went to take a closer look, and then suddenly I was here."

"Gabi must be worried about you."

"I wish. But we all promised to be quiet and not bother the bats, so I doubt he's even noticed that I'm not there."

"And Matt?"

"I don't know."

"Do you see your flashlight anywhere?"

Sari was quiet for a moment.

"No."

"Try and be brave like when we saw the jackals. I'll go get some rope."

Josh ran over to the Scouts' backpacks, hoping to find the rope they'd used at the campsite. It wasn't there. He realized it must be with the equipment they'd left on the bus.

Should he tell Sari to wait for Gabi and the others to rescue her, or try to save her himself? As Josh looked at the backpacks, he had an idea. Unfastening the bags one by one, he pulled out sweaters, long-sleeved shirts, jeans, and socks. Scooping them into his arms, he ran back to the hole.

Josh took a pair of jeans and tied one sweater sleeve to one leg and another sweater sleeve to the other leg, then tied a few shirtsleeves together to make a ladder long enough to reach into the hole. He pulled the knots as tight as he could.

The hard part was finding a way to tie one end around the tree. The clothes were too unwieldy.

Josh groaned. He knew this wasn't going to end well, but he had no choice. Unhooking the belt that Amit had given him, he folded the top of his pants over twice to keep them from slipping down. As long as he didn't move around too much, the pants would stay up. Wrapping his belt around the tree gave him a secure anchor for the sleeve of the rope ladder.

"Josh?" Sari called.

"Hang on," said Josh. "I'm almost ready."

He lowered the clothes ladder into the hole.

Josh felt Sari pull on the end and heard her laugh. "Dana's going to kill you!" she said. "This is her favorite shirt."

"You'll have to blow out the candle before you start climbing," Josh reminded her. Josh hitched up his pants again and lay down beside the hole.

Suddenly the makeshift ladder grew taut as Sari tried to find her footing and started to climb. "Keep going," Josh called. He clutched the end of the jeans and hoped that the knots would hold. He heard Sari breathing heavily.

"Come on," he said. "You're almost here."

"I'm slipping," Sari cried. The rope went slack.

"You were so close." Josh squinted through the darkness. "Try again. Bring your knees up and wrap them around the knots. Just keep climbing until I can reach your hand."

Josh held the ladder steady. He heard Sari grunt with each pull. Finally, he saw her arm. He seized her wrist.

"Come on, Sari. Take my other hand."

As her fingers wrapped around Josh's, they clung tightly to one another, but Sari's weight started pulling his body forward. Josh felt his grasp weakening. He dug his toes into the ground.

"We can do this, Sari. Pull!"

"I'm trying."

Josh slid forward another few inches. He was losing strength. He was getting dragged into the hole! At any moment he was going to tumble in head first!

CHAPTER 13

Before he could even let out a scream, Josh shot forward. Instinctively, he tucked in his chin and protected his head with his hands. Moments later he hit the ground, just missing Sari.

"Are you hurt?" asked Sari.

Josh sat up. He was still in one piece—and still had his pants on. "I'm good."

"That was some somersault," said Sari. "But what're we going to do now?"

"I don't know. Wow, it's dark down here. Do you still have the candle?"

"I think you landed on it."

Josh groped beneath him and found the candle, but it was broken. He pulled out another one from his pocket and struck a match.

"That's better," said Sari. "Now I can see you."

"This hole smells really bad, no offense," said Josh.

"It's bat pee."

"If you say so."

Josh pulled on his ladder. It was still tied to the tree and seemed secure. He stood and yanked up his pants. "We'll try again."

Gripping the clothes with his right hand above the first knot, Josh clamped his left hand above it. Like a monkey, he lifted himself off the ground and wrapped his knees around the ladder, crossing his ankles with the knotted clothes between them.

He grasped the ladder above the next knot and followed with his other hand.

"You're a natural," said Sari. She held the candle while Josh climbed. Slowly he made his way up, not looking down, not thinking about what would happen if a knot slipped.

The air became fresher. The light grew stronger. Josh was almost at the opening. Pushing his head through the hole, he clutched the bushes. He couldn't believe it. He was almost out! He'd actually climbed his way out of a hole using a ladder he'd made all by himself. But as he slithered forward, his pants started slipping!

"Oh noooo—"

"What's wrong?" Sari called.

"Nothing. Almost there." Josh squeezed his knees together to keep his pants from falling off. He couldn't let go of the bush without tumbling back into the hole. He inched forward, and his pants slid lower.

He had to make a choice.

Josh tugged himself out onto solid ground.

"You made—Josh?" Sari paused. "Ahh, I think you dropped something."

Josh scooted around, staying close to the ground, and looked down the hole at Sari.

"Tell me these aren't your pants and that they're part of the ladder."

Josh groaned. "Could you hurry and get up here, and could you bring my pants with you? It's kind of drafty without them."

"No," said Sari. "I'm laughing too hard."

"Hurry!" said Josh. "Before everyone gets here!" He couldn't bear to think about what Roy would say if they caught Josh in his underwear.

The ladder grew taut. Josh held it steady.

"Use your knees to help support yourself."

Sari grunted in reply.

"Almost here!" he encouraged her. As he saw the top of Sari's head, Josh lunged for her wrist.

"Don't let go," cried Sari.

"I've got you," said Josh.

"And so do I," said Matt, catching Sari's other hand. "Let's pull together, Josh. One, two, three."

"We did it!" said Sari, as she scrambled out waving Josh's pants in the air.

"I'm impressed," said Matt, brushing the dirt off his hands.

"Give me those," said Josh, grabbing his pants and trying to pull them on quickly over his navy blue briefs.

Just then, Tomer and Amit came running up. "Hey, Josh, Sari. What's going on?" asked Tomer. He looked at the clothes ladder and at Josh holding up his pants. "Wow, can I try climbing down?"

"Hold on there, Sport," said Matt, untying Josh's belt from the tree. "Here, Josh. You might want this."

"Ya think?" said Sari, trying not to giggle.

Tomer and Amit knelt down above the hole. "Gabi almost had a heart attack when he saw that Sari wasn't with us when we left the cave," said Amit. "What happened?"

"Long story," Josh mumbled, threading his belt through his pant loops.

Dana ran up. "You both could use some of these," she said, offering them wet wipes.

Josh rubbed off a ton of dirt. "Thanks," he said.

Gabi arrived a moment later, panting heavily. "Sari!" he said. "We were so worried. I doubled back through the cave once I realized you weren't with us."

"Sorry, Gabi. It was an accident. But Josh rescued me."

Nate and Roy were the last to arrive, and Sari repeated the story all over again.

"What a mess," said Gabi, noticing all the clothes, and the contents of their packs strewn across the ground.

"I had to use what there was," said Josh. "The ropes are on the bus."

Roy showed off his sweater. "That's some knot." He untied it from the jeans and pulled it on. One sleeve hung down to his knees, stretched out of proportion. Josh waited for Roy to explode. "You used my sweater as the main link," said Roy.

"Yeah," said Josh. "Sorry it got stretched out like that."

"Sorry? This is great! It'll make a fantastic story. I can't wait to tell Baruch and my mom."

"You're not mad?" asked Josh.

"I'm only mad I didn't stay behind with you! The bats were sleeping and the cave was pretty boring."

Josh laughed. His time outside the cave had been anything but boring.

"You were really resourceful," said Gabi, as he inspected the knot in his shirtsleeve. "I think you've just invented the clothes hitch."

"Ha ha!" said Nate.

Amit, Tomer and Nate slapped, clapped and gave a thumbs-up.

"Couldn't have done it without you showing me those knots yesterday," Josh said to Gabi. "Teamwork," he added.

Nate put his arm around his brother. "Way to go, Josh! Sari told me how you saved her. It sounded really frightening – enough to scare the pants off you."

Josh punched Nate's arm. "Not funny," he said.

"Hey, Gabi," said Nate. "I think you should forgive Josh since he's been so brave."

Gabi nodded. "He sure has."

The Scouts cheered.

CHAPTER 14

"You can have the seat next to the window," said Dana, scooting over. "I know you like watching the scenery."

"Thanks," said Josh, who caught Matt's smile as he sat down. "Everything's so different here from at home."

As Josh looked out the window, he heard the others chatting and singing. After a while he realized that Dana was sitting quietly, not joining in.

"Are you okay?" asked Josh.

"I'm fine. I was thinking about how you saved Sari. It was—"

Josh was hoping she'd say brave, daring, totally Super Scout.

"Selfless," she said.

"Selfless?"

"Yeah. I mean, you didn't think about how danger-ous it was to rescue Sari or what would have happened if we'd found all our stuff ruined and Sari still in the hole."

"That would've been really hard to explain. Sorry about your shirt."

"No biggie," she said.

"You need to grow really long arms, use it as a swing, or toss it."

"No way. Now it's a souvenir." She paused. "I couldn't have done what you did. If I'd been left behind, Sari would still be in the hole."

"We would've all pulled her out eventually," said Josh. "And if she'd stayed there, it would be because you made her feel like it was the best place to be. You would've reminded her how much she loves nature, and how much she knows. You would've encouraged her to collect a bunch of samples of caustic rock."

Dana laughed. "You're funny. Not 'Nate' funny, nice funny." She fell silent again. Then, "I'm just not good at doing things like everyone else. I can't even cook as well as Roy. We'd be eating tomato sauce out of the can, if it were me in charge."

Josh had to admit that was true. Dana wasn't into nature like Sari. She couldn't climb trees like Tomer. She didn't know all the songs that Amit knew. "But you are good at something," said Josh.

"What?"

"Your English is really good."

"My mom's taught me a lot of languages. She knows Braille, too. She teaches kids who are visually impaired. My mom says that there're lots of ways of seeing people, not only with our eyes."

"Oh," said Josh. "That's why—"

"Why what?"

"Why you see things—" he paused, thinking how to say it— "about ourselves that we don't realize. Like what you said about me jumping in to help Nate. You see us with more than just your eyes."

Dana looked up from her shirt. "You think so?"

"I know so."

Dana giggled, and Josh thought she even blushed, but before he could say anything else, she joined in the chorus of a song that Josh didn't know. He turned to look out the window again, feeling good about himself. Selfless. When he was trying to get Sari out of the hole, he hadn't worried about what Gabi and the others would say; he just thought about how scared Sari was and how he needed to help her. Kind and selfless were almost better than brave or daring.

Soon they pulled into the parking lot by the entrance to the Bell Caves. Gabi told them to fill their water bottles and asked Josh to come with him to the ticket desk, where he could find a brochure in English.

"Sorry," the woman in the ticket office said when it was their turn. She turned to the others standing in line. "The caves are full. We can't let in anyone else today. You'll have to come back tomorrow."

"But my son has been so excited about this part of the trip. I don't want to disappoint him," said a woman with a young boy who looked about five years old.

"We made reservations," said Gabi. "You can't turn us away."

The worker sighed and shrugged. "I don't make the rules. I just enforce them. We have a limited number of people we allow in. We didn't expect so many tourists at this time of year." She turned to Gabi. "The Scouts are booked for tomorrow. I'm sorry. There must have been a mistake, but there's nothing I can do. There are too many people inside."

"Bar Kochba's whole army hid out in those caves," Josh said to Gabi. "And she's telling us there isn't enough room for a group of Scouts and a few more tourists?"

The worker looked at Josh. "I heard that. Bar Kochba doesn't set the rules now, the Archaeology Society does. Bar Kochba wasn't worried about preserving the tunnels for research. Standing around here won't change anything. Again, I'm sorry. Now, please, move on."

"To where?" asked Gabi. "I've got a bus full of Scouts."

"You could try the caves at Luzit. They're not far from here. They're very similar, and they won't be as crowded. Most people don't know about them."

"That's not a bad idea," said Gabi. He ushered the other Scout counselors into a huddle. It took them only seconds to decide.

"Get back on the bus!" called Gabi. "We're going to Luzit."

Everyone cheered. As Josh climbed on board, he felt a tug on his pant leg and saw the boy who had been standing in line with his mother.

"I want to go with you," said the boy. He had tied his mother's scarf around his neck as if it were a Scout's neckerchief.

"You're too young to be a Scout," said Josh.

The boy's mother was standing nearby, smiling at Josh. "I heard you speaking English before. I wonder if you can help us. Could you ask your Scout leader if we can join you?"

Josh walked the woman and boy over to Gabi. "This lady would like to ask you something," said Josh. "This is Gabi. He speaks English, too."

"May we join you?" she asked. "We're flying home to Florida tomorrow, and I promised Yoni that I'd show him the biggest cave ever. I never imagined the caves would be unavailable." She patted her son on the top of his head. "I'd hate to disappoint him."

Gabi frowned. "I'm sorry, but we don't have any room on the bus."

"We have a car, but we don't know where the other caves are situated. We won't bother you. We'll just follow behind at a distance."

"I guess that's okay," said Gabi. "You're welcome to follow us. Glad to be of help."

When they stopped at Luzit, Roy was the first to get off the bus. "Hey, I know this place. Baruch and my mother took me here last summer. Come on, everyone. The trail to the caves is this way. I'll show you how to find them."

"Slow down a second, Roy. I'm in charge here, remember?" said Gabi, catching Roy by the arm.

"Hey, let go," said Roy.

Gabi loosened his grip. "I know you've been everywhere, Roy, and I'm sure you can be helpful, but before we explore these caves, I need to sit with the other counselors and check out a few maps."

After the previous night, Josh thought maps and a few reconnaissance trips wouldn't be a bad thing.

"You don't need maps," Roy scoffed. "I could take you through the caves and tunnels blindfolded."

"I'm sure Gabi and the other leaders will be glad to have you help them, Roy," said Matt. "But you have to let Gabi do his job."

Roy frowned, but seemed to accept the situation. A few minutes later Gabi came back with a worried expression. "I don't like this," he said. "We usually check out the site before we lead a group inside. Who knows if the rain, archaeologists, or antiquity robbers haven't changed the inside completely?"

"The worker at the Bell Caves said it'd be fine," said Josh.

"True," Gabi agreed. "So we're going in, but we have to stay close to one another. No one wanders off."

"Hey," said Sari. "I learned my lesson!"

Josh gazed at the uncultivated land that stretched out before him. The grass was even lush in places. Sari had said it was because of natural water wells. It seemed so calm and untouched. But underneath, Josh knew, there were miles of mazes and tunnels that turned in and spiraled down into hidden caves, places where the Jews had held their secret meetings, planned their strategies, and stayed hidden from the Romans in ancient times.

"I sure hope Gabi knows what he's doing," Nate said to Josh. "Because if Roy takes charge—"

"We'll be in big trouble," said Josh.

CHAPTER 15

"Come on, Josh," Nate called as he sat down at the top of the cave's entrance. "Think Water Park, only this slide is rocks and dirt. Watch me!"

Nate pushed himself off.

When Josh saw that Nate had made it to the bottom, he sat down and followed. It was a smooth ride into an enormous pit with a domed ceiling some 50 feet above him. Streaks of sunlight filtered in through the hole, giving the cave a light and airy feeling, not at all like what he'd experienced before.

"This is incredible," said Josh, his voice bouncing off the walls and echoing back to him. "It's the most gigantic cave I've ever seen." Staring up at the cave's ceiling as he walked, he collided with Sari. "Sorry."

"That's okay," she said. "I wasn't watching where I was going either. This cave is perfectly round, like a huge upside-down bell."

"That's why it's called a bell cave, ding-dong," said Roy. "The dome was man-made."

"And probably woman-made," said Sari.

"Man or woman, it was made long before there were cranes and jackhammers," said Tomer.

"Deep, isn't it?" Roy's voice echoed, bounced and re-echoed off the cave walls as if there were many Roys.

"Now that's what I call acoustics," said Sari. "If my brother knew about this, he'd want to bring his band here. They could really kick up some sound."

"There'd only be bats around to hear them," said Roy.

"Yeah, I can smell their pee," said Dana.

"There're thousands, and even tens of thousands of them, in these caves," said Roy. "Bats hang out together. They're social animals."

"Anyone ready to leave now?" said Dana. "I've had enough hanging out with bats for one day."

"This way," called Gabi.

Josh followed close to Gabi. He wanted to learn everything about the cave. It was magical, beautiful, and terrifying at the same time.

"Ugh," said Amit, stepping into a mound of pigeon poop.

"They say it's good luck," said Sari.

"When it drops on you," said Dana. "Not when you step in it."

"The next cave we'll come to was used as a columbarium," said Gabi.

"More remains of dead people?" asked Dana.

"No," said Gabi. "Columbarium comes from the Latin word for dove. It's a place where they used to keep pigeons. The holes on the cave walls are where the pigeons nested."

"Looks like they still think this is their home," said Nate, scraping his shoe on the side of a rock.

"Okay, Scouts," said Gabi. "Before we continue, let's stop here to have a short snack. After we eat, we'll explore a bit more and then head back for our last night."

"We'll have so much fun later," Amit told Josh. "There's a big bonfire and there's also a Scout ceremony where new members are sworn in. We roast marshmallows too, and tell stories."

"And since tonight is the last night of Hanukkah, we light all the candles," said Dana. "It'll be great."

Josh couldn't wait. It sounded like the perfect end to a perfect trip.

CHAPTER 16

"I think you've all learned a good lesson about leaving food around," said Gabi. He had managed to rustle up a snack, taking cucumbers from one group, pita from another, and hummus, pickles, and tomatoes from the counselors' supply.

Dana unfolded a paper table cloth and laid it in the center of the circle. "I don't want pigeon poop in my sandwich."

Josh took a pita and stuffed it with hummus. It tasted pretty good. He'd hoped for peanut butter, but knew better than to mention it. He caught Nate frowning and figured he was thinking the same thing. Amit, Tomer, Dana, Sari, and Roy scooped up the hummus as if it were from the last jar of peanut butter on the supermarket shelf.

"Me and Baruch rappelled into these caves last year," said Roy, his mouth full.

"No way," said Tomer. "That hole is, like, sixty feet above us."

"And I rappelled all the way down by myself. If you don't believe me, call and ask Baruch."

"How'd you do it?" asked Amit.

"We tied our ropes around the tall rocks near the rim," said Roy, pointing to the hole at the top of the dome. "Baruch put a harness around me, and I lowered myself all the way into where we are now."

Tomer whistled. "Rappellin' Roy! Wasn't it frightening to hang that high above the ground?"

"At first, but I got used to it." Roy laughed. "When I'm a paratrooper in the army, sixty feet will seem like nothing. I'll be jumping from planes."

"That's some goal," said Gabi.

"Imagine," said Josh, "if Bar Kochba had had a squadron of planes. He would've beaten the Romans in a flash." Josh gazed up at the ceiling. "Maybe they didn't have harnesses and nylon ropes, but if they could make a bell cave like this one and build cities from the rocks around here, I bet they figured out how to rappel."

The Scouts fell silent as they ate.

"What's up, Nate?" asked Amit, passing him some olives. "Did you run out of jokes?"

Nate shrugged. "I was going to tell the one about the kids who brought pizza to the bat cave – but it's too cheesy. And the only other ones I can think of down here are so old, they're pre-hysterical."

Amit rolled his eyes as the others slapped, clapped and gave him a thumbs-up.

Gabi filled another pita with hummus. "We can learn a lot about our history from what was left behind. They say that there are more than two thousand of these caves around here. We've only discovered a fraction of them. The ancient Jews didn't use these caves only for gathering stones. They built olive presses and water cisterns down here too."

"So there must be tons of tunnels," said Nate.

"Zillions," said Roy.

Josh shivered. He'd left his sweater on the bus. "And these caves have great air-conditioning. It was getting really hot outside, and now—"

"I'm cold too," said Sari, pulling on a sweater.

"Then it's time to pack up and explore," said Gabi. "And here's the rule. You can walk around in here, but absolutely no going inside any of the tunnels. Okay, Scouts. We reconvene in fifteen minutes."

"This cave is marvelous," said Yoni's mom, who had come to thank Gabi for letting them tag along. "It's hard to believe that two thousand years ago there was a whole city down here."

"With giants," said Yoni. "That's why the roof is so high. A giant made that hole with his head when he stood up."

"And the underground tunnels were for the monster mice that lived with the giant," said Josh.

Yoni's eyes grew as big as pitas. "Do you think there're still monster mice inside the tunnels?"

Josh shrugged. "Do you think there's still a giant who lives here?"

Yoni slipped his hand into his mother's. "Come on, Mommy. I want to crawl inside the tunnels."

Yoni and his mother waved goodbye as they walked toward the entrance of an adjoining cave. Gabi reminded everyone not to stray too far.

Josh was about to follow Nate and Tomer when a cry echoed through the cave.

"What was that?" asked Sari.

The cry sounded a second time, louder and shriller, followed by a shout: "Yoni!"

CHAPTER 17

Everyone gathered around Yoni's mother. She stood by the entrance to the next cave, clutching her bag and shivering uncontrollably.

"What's wrong?" asked Gabi. "Where's Yoni?"

Yoni's mother grabbed Gabi's arm. "Yoni wanted to crawl inside the cave to see the monster mice in the tunnels. I told him he couldn't, since I'm too big to follow him. I turned away for a second, and he was gone." She caught her breath, struggling to speak through her tears.

"Yoni!" Gabi shouted.

Yoni's mother tightened her grasp on Gabi and shook him. "You've got to do something!" She turned to them. Her eyes were wide and glazed with fear. "Please, help me find him!"

"Roy!" barked Gabi. "Come here. Now."

Roy rushed over.

"Are the tunnels through this hole the same ones you and Baruch explored last year?"

Roy nodded. "The tunnel Yoni went down splits into two forks beyond the entrance. That's as far as we went. Baruch was wearing a backpack, and the tunnel got too narrow for him to continue. Actually, I went on a bit by myself."

Gabi hesitated, then turned to Yoni's mother. "I'm going to go call the other counselors."

Yoni's mother wouldn't release Gabi. "No. We can't waste any time. The deeper Yoni crawls, the harder it will be to find him. You have to go after him. Now! He probably hasn't gone very far. You can still catch him if you hurry."

Josh thought she was right. They had to move fast to try and catch Yoni before he took too many twists and turns. What if he spiraled into a bottomless pit?

"I'll go," said Josh.

"No. I will," said Gabi.

"You can't," said Josh. "If Baruch couldn't fit through the tunnel, then you won't either." Josh paused. "Maybe Roy can come with me since he's been in the tunnels before."

"You want me to go with you?" asked Roy.

And as if they'd been planning for this moment, everyone snapped into position. Sari took off her sweater and draped it over Yoni's mother's shoulders.

"Take my health bar," said Dana. "If Yoni's scared, it might distract him."

"Give Josh your flashlight, Tomer," said Nate. He paused. "And Josh, be careful!"

"Josh is great at crawling through tunnels," Josh heard Amit say to Yoni's mother. "Roy is fearless."

Gabi turned to both boys. "Don't lose sight of each other. Don't go too far in. If anything looks dangerous, get out. The rest of you stay here while I go for help."

"Don't worry, we'll find him," Josh said to Yoni's mother. He wished he hadn't mentioned the monster mice earlier.

She wiped her face with a tissue. "Please hurry!"

Josh scurried inside the cave. The floor was smooth near the entrance. It had been worn down by the many curious tourists who had braved the first few meters of the dark and narrow passageway.

"Wait, Josh!" a muffled voice called to him. "You should've let me go first," said Roy. "I know the way."

"It's too late to switch places now," said Josh. He'd been in such a hurry that he hadn't thought to let Roy lead. "I'll tell you when we come to the fork. Just stay close."

"Am right behind you," said Roy.

"Yoni!" shouted Josh. "Where are you?"

Josh bumped his head on a slab of rock that jutted out from the wall. He cursed himself, but kept crawling as fast as he could. He called Yoni's name again. Still no answer. He paused to catch his breath and listen.

"Roy?"

No answer. Josh's heart dropped to his stomach. He wanted to turn around, but there was no room to maneuver. Where was Roy? Why wasn't he behind him?

"Roy!" he called louder.

"I'm here," Roy said, panting. "My shoelace came undone and my shoe fell off."

Josh tried to imagine putting on his own shoe. He would have had to reverse, grab the shoe, and then flip over, lie on his back, and pull his knees up to his chest to reach his foot. "How did you get it on?"

"I didn't," said Roy. "I left it there. We can collect it on the way out. Let's keep moving."

Josh wanted to speed up but, at the same time knew he had to move carefully. He didn't know what surprises lay ahead. A few moments later, they arrived at a fork. Josh shined his flashlight into both tunnels and strained his ears.

"Yoni! Where are you?" Josh shouted. Silence.

"Which way?" Josh asked Roy.

Roy hesitated. "I went right last time, but we don't know if Yoni went that way."

Josh crawled into the right fork. "Yoni!" he called again, pausing to brush off a few pebbles that had become embedded in the palm of his hand.

As they crawled along, desperate to find some clue that Yoni was ahead, Roy said, "My mom's boyfriend—"

"Baruch," said Josh.

"Yeah, him, he said that these tunnels are always being dug up by archaeologists, or by grave robbers hoping to find archaeological treasure that they can sell or keep as souvenirs." Roy's breathing became heavier. "I don't see any trace of Yoni. Maybe we should've taken the left-hand fork instead. Maybe we're not going the right way."

CHAPTER 18

As Roy panted behind Josh, they hit another split in the tunnel.

"Which way now?" asked Josh.

Roy didn't answer.

"Roy?" Josh called. The air was dense. His lungs felt like they were packed with layer upon layer of fine dusty chalk that had fallen from the ceiling.

"Still right behind you," said Roy. "I think we should turn back."

"We can't. What about Yoni?"

"Maybe Gabi's found him already. He said he was going for help."

Josh considered that possibility and shook his head. "Not enough time has gone by." Besides, though he couldn't explain why, he had a feeling that Yoni had been through there.

Josh flashed his light down both tunnels to weigh his options. He'd chosen to lead. It was his responsibility to decide which fork to take. Going back would be like telling Yoni's mother they'd given up, that there was no hope in ever finding Yoni in the maze of tunnels. Sure, he was scared, but the thought of Yoni alone and trapped somewhere forced him to persevere. They had to continue.

Josh decided to go right. This way they'd know to always turn left on their way back. But what if the right way was really the wrong way?

Josh's head spun.

"Well?" said Roy. "What do you think?"

"You take the right fork and I'll take the left one," said Josh.

"What about the buddy system? Gabi said we should stick together."

"I'm not crazy about my idea, either," said Josh. "Leave your shoe at the mouth of the right fork to remind me which way you went. I'll kick mine off farther on. If I have to take another fork, I'll leave my shoe and a sock as a marker. You do the same. If you find Yoni, yell as loud as you can."

"I've already dropped one shoe."

"I know." Josh paused. "If you'd rather turn around, I understand. You can tell Gabi where I am."

"And leave you on your own? Hey, we're Scouts! We stick together."

Josh couldn't believe Roy was being so loyal after all that had happened before now, but whatever the reason, it was all good. After a few seconds, Josh heard Roy grunt as he removed his other shoe. "There. I've left my shoe, and I'm on my way. Josh?"

"Yeah?"

"Nothing," said Roy.

"What?"

"Of all the Scouts, you chose me to go with you. No one ever chooses me."

"You were the best Scout for the job," said Josh. "We can do this together."

"You bet!" said Roy, sounding more convinced.

As soon as Roy was gone, Josh called out for Yoni. "It's me. Josh. Your mom wants you. She sent me in here to get you. If you can hear me, answer. Please!"

Josh didn't expect an answer. But then he heard some kind of sound. Was it his shoe scraping along the floor of the tunnel? Josh listened so intently, he thought his eardrums might burst.

He heard the sound again.

It was a whimper, like a wounded puppy might make. And it was coming from somewhere nearby.

"Yoni?"

"Help," said a small voice. "I'm lost."

Then Josh heard crying. It was rising from somewhere below him.

He paused, feeling the ground ahead of him before pressing forward.

Yoni's whimpers grew louder, until Josh felt like he was right above him. As he moved another inch forward his hand touched the entrance to a cave. Josh flashed his light inside. He couldn't believe it. Yoni was huddling at the bottom of a slippery rocky slide.

"Roy!" shouted Josh over his shoulder. "Yoni's here." Then to Yoni, he yelled, "Are you okay?"

"No. I wanna to go home."

"I hear you, Buddy. That's why I'm here. I'll come get you." Josh waved the beam of his flashlight around to determine how deep it was beyond where Yoni was sitting, but he couldn't see much.

"My mom must be really mad at me."

"She's not mad; she's worried."

"I'm scared." Yoni started to cry louder and harder.

"Think how brave you were to come this far," said Josh. "You're in an ancient fortress where people lived thousands of years ago." Josh maneuvered around as he spoke. He wanted to try lowering himself into the cave. He hoped there were some stepping stones, like in the cistern, to make it easier to get down the slope.

"I'm hungry," said Yoni, his sobs subsiding.

"As soon as we get back, we'll have a big party with

lots of yummy things to eat. I've got a treat in my pocket just for you."

"Josh?" It was Roy.

"Over here! Yoni's in a cave below where I'm sitting."

"You found him!" said Roy, crawling up behind Josh.

"I want to go home," said Yoni. He started to holler.

"I know," said Josh. "Here's my friend Roy. We've come to get you. Right, Roy?"

"Right," said Roy. "How does it look, Josh?"

As Josh shined his flashlight inside, he couldn't see even a ledge to help him lower himself in. It was going to be one slippery slope all the way down.

CHAPTER 19

"Once you hit the ground, I don't see any way to climb back up," said Roy.

"I know," said Josh. "I think I should slide down and stay with Yoni while you go get Gabi. Ask him for a rope ladder and a stronger flashlight."

"Sure thing," said Roy.

"We'll need to find a way to secure the ladder. See if you can bring a pole that's longer than the length of the hole of the entrance. We can wind the rope ladder around the middle of it and secure the ends of the pole against the sides of the entrance so it doesn't slip."

"Right," said Roy.

"And Roy?" said Josh.

"Yeah?"

"Hurry."

"I'll be back before you know it," Roy promised. "But I need you to lend me your flashlight. Mine has no battery left."

Josh hesitated. He didn't want to be left without a light, but he knew that Roy needed it more than he did. "Okay," said Josh. "I have some candles. Move, Yoni. Here I come."

Josh sat down on the edge of the rim, took a deep breath and pushed himself off, sliding down into the hole.

"Yoni?"

"I'm here." He touched Josh's arm.

"That was fun," said Josh. He reached into his pocket. "Hey, no more crying. I'll light a candle." Josh struck a match and lit one of the Hanukkah candles. The cave filled with light. He lifted the candle higher to get a better view of his surroundings. They were in a small room that had been carefully chiseled out. Lining the sides of the walls were low, narrow slabs of rock.

"You okay?" asked Roy from above.

"I'm fine." Josh stretched his arms above his head. "The distance from the ground to the entrance is an extra few feet from the tips of my fingers," Josh called to Roy.

"Got it," said Roy. "We'll find a ladder that's the right size and have you both out of there before you know it."

"This place looks like it was someone's living room," Josh told Yoni.

"Is that where they slept?" asked Yoni, pointing to the slabs.

"Could be."

Yoni's silence was punctuated by a few sobs, but finally he quieted down.

"Can I have a candle too?" he asked.

"Let's save it for when this one burns out."

Shielding the flame to keep it from flickering, Josh imagined the Jewish warriors on their way through the maze of tunnels, stopping in this room to plan their next battle or to regroup.

Josh let Yoni take the candle. "Hold it up straight," he said. "Help will be here soon."

Not even a miracle could make the candle last forever. He spotted a spider about to crawl onto Yoni's leg and quickly brushed it off. He found a rock and showed Yoni how to tip some wax on it. Josh set the bottom of the candle in the wax so it could stand on its own.

"What did the people who lived here do all day?" asked Yoni.

"They built things."

Yoni rested his head against Josh's arm. Josh leaned against the wall to get more comfortable.

"And what did they do at night? There's no TV or computer."

"They told stories, I guess," said Josh. "And ate snacks." Josh took out the treat Dana had given him and offered it to Yoni.

"Thank you," said Yoni. "What kind of stories did they tell? Do you know any?"

"Once upon a time," Josh began, clearing his throat.

"I don't like fairy tales," said Yoni. "Tell me a real story."

"It's not a fairy tale," said Josh, wondering if he knew anything else besides Jack and the Beanstalk, Cinderella, and Hansel and Gretel. A story about giants would be too scary. Cinderella was a wimp, and Hansel and Gretel got lost and a witch wanted to eat them. Then Josh remembered the story Gabi had told them inside the cistern.

"Once upon a time," Josh repeated, "there was a very wise rabbi who had a daughter who he loved a lot."

"What happened to him?" asked Yoni. "Did he get lost in a cave?"

"No," said Josh. "He wanted to help his daughter find someone to marry who was both clever and wise. So, together, they thought up a riddle. The rabbi said that whoever solved the riddle could marry his daughter."

Yoni munched on the health bar. "What if she didn't like him and didn't want to marry him?"

"He had to be smart, but of course she had to like him, too."

"What was the riddle?"

"The rabbi and his daughter lived near a cave," Josh

continued. "They knew how dark and lonely caves could be. They said that whoever brought something that could fill the cave completely could ask to marry the rabbi's daughter."

Yoni sat up. "This cave?"

Josh shrugged. "Maybe it was this cave. The first man to arrive brought a load of rocks. He worked for hours hauling stones, rolling boulders, and packing the cave from floor to ceiling with all the rocks he could find."

"And did he win?"

Josh shook his head. "No. When the rabbi arrived, he looked inside and said, 'There are spaces between these rocks. You've not succeeded.'"

"The candle's going out," said Yoni.

"That's okay," said Josh. "I have another one." He watched as the last bit of wax melted. What was taking Roy so long? Maybe he got lost going back. What if Gabi and whatever help he'd found couldn't reach them?

"What did they do next?" asked Yoni.

"They waited. Another man came and said he wanted to try. He filled the cave with feathers. He brought feathers from peacocks and pigeons and roosters and geese, and packed the cave from ceiling to floor and from side to side with piles and piles of feathers."

Yoni sneezed.

"Watch the flame!" said Josh.

"Sorry," said Yoni. "Thinking about the feathers made my nose tickle. Did he win?"

Josh shook his head. "No. The daughter said, 'Feathers are lighter than rocks and very pretty, but once they settle they won't reach the top of the cave. You have not succeeded.'"

"Too bad," said Yoni. "Then what?"

"A third man came. The man wasn't pulling a wagon filled with rocks, or carrying sacks filled with feathers."

"What did he have?" asked Yoni.

"Nothing."

"Nothing?"

The man said, "Come with me into the cave and give me the candle that's in your hand."

"Then what did he do?"

"He blew out the light," said Josh, leaning toward the flame.

"Don't blow out ours!" said Yoni.

"No way!" said Josh, taking out his last candle and lighting it from the flame of the other one. He set it down. "When the man blew out the candle, there was darkness. The rabbi and his daughter waited. They could feel that this man had something special about him that the other men didn't have. A few seconds later the man lit the candle, and, whoosh! The cave filled up with light!"

Yoni clapped his hands. "He did it! He did it!"

"No," said Josh, his eye still on the candle that was burning too quickly. Soon he and Yoni would be sitting in pitch darkness. "The rabbi's daughter was not about to let him win so easily. She blew out the candle."

"Oh no!" said Yoni. "Why'd she do that?"

Josh paused. "The rabbi's daughter thought the man was smart, but she wanted to test how smart. She said, "The candle is mine and so was the match you used to light it. Although your candle filled this cave with light, our instructions were to bring something with you which could fill up the cave. You've brought nothing of your own."

"Oh," said Yoni. "So he lost, too."

"No," said Josh. "This man was a very smart man. He knew that not only things fill up spaces, but ideas do, too. He had many ideas, enough to fill many caves, but he wasn't sure they would agree to that solution either. So he sat in the dark and pondered the problem. And just as the rabbi and his daughter were about to leave, the man started to do a very strange thing."

"What?" said Yoni, tilting his head to see Josh's face.

"He started to sing."

"Sing? Why?"

"I'll show you." Then Josh, in a tiny voice, since he was never very good at singing, started to hum the only Hanukkah song he knew.

"Maoz Tzur…"

It came out wobbly at first, but then his voice grew stronger. Yoni joined in, and soon the cave was resounding and rebounding with the sound of their voices, which rose and rose and grew louder and louder.

And as their song filled the empty cave, and there was hardly any flame left, Josh tightened his arm around Yoni's shoulder, hoping that their voices would be heard above the cave, through the tunnel and all the way into the huge Bell Cave, where Yoni's mother, Gabi, and all the Scouts were waiting.

"I hear them!" Roy's voice echoed from above.

"We're here!" shouted Josh.

"We're here!" echoed Yoni.

CHAPTER 20

Nate was the first to pop his head into the hole. "Ahoy down there!" he said, shining his flashlight on them. "Hey, Yoni, what do you call a bear with no teeth? A gummy bear! And guess what, your mom gave me a whole bunch for you."

"Am I glad to see you," said Josh, as Nate pointed the flashlight at himself.

"I'm here too," said Dana. "Move, Nate. I want to see."

"He's my brother," said Nate, "so I should go down first."

"We're all here," said Amit. "Except for Gabi, because he couldn't fit."

Within seconds there was a whoosh and Nate landed beside them, followed by Tomer, Dana, Sari, and Amit. Nate gave Josh an awkward hug. Josh thought the cave seemed much bigger and warmer with everyone inside.

"Wait," said Josh. "Where's Roy? And if you're all here, how're we going to get back up?"

"We brought a rope ladder," Roy called from above. "Sari helped us make one really fast. We measured Nate and then found a pole long enough to hang the ladder from."

"Good thing we're twins," said Nate.

"Yoni," said Dana. "Your mom is waiting outside the cave. She says to give you a big hug."

Roy let down the rope ladder. "I'll test it out, Yoni," said Josh. "All you have to do is follow me."

"But I'm scared," said Yoni.

"I'll be right behind you. Just hold on tight to the rungs," said Nate. "Don't forget what the nose said to the finger."

Yoni took a step. "What did the nose say to the finger?" asked Yoni, as he moved another rung.

"Stop picking on me!"

"Huh?" said Yoni. "Noses can't talk."

"Never mind," said Nate. "Now start climbing."

"Good for you, Yoni!" said Josh, as Yoni reached the top.

"I did it," said Yoni.

"We all did," said Josh.

"Teamwork," said Roy, punching Josh on the shoulder.

Josh led the way through the tunnel, following the signposts they'd left earlier. When they crawled out into the Bell Cave, shouts of laughter and applause resounded loudly as Yoni's mother scooped Yoni into a bear hug. Then she hugged Josh so tightly he thought she'd never let go.

"She did the same thing to me," said Roy.

Gabi shook Josh's hand. "Great job!" he said. Then he rested his arm on Roy's shoulder. "You boys really pulled it off. Roy, your mom and Baruch will be soooo proud of you."

"My dad would've been too," said Roy.

"Without a doubt," said Gabi. "Now let's move, Scouts."

They ran out of the cave, glad to return to ground level.

"Where are the other Scouts?" asked Josh.

"They went to prepare the bonfire for tonight," said Amit. "They said they'd get everything ready for the celebration while we rescued Yoni."

Yoni wrapped his arms around Josh. "Thank you," he said.

"Any time," said Josh. "Just not any time too soon."

The Scouts waved goodbye and climbed onto the bus. It was growing dark. Josh was too tired even to look out the window. He was sure he'd fall asleep in seconds.

"I was never so frightened in my life," said Dana, who'd plopped down on the empty seat beside him. "That poor kid, to think what could've happened to him if we hadn't got him out."

"Once Roy and I found Yoni, I knew you guys would come through for us," said Josh.

"And we did! Sari showed us how to do another kind of quick knot that never slips. Sari said I was the best at tying them and had me do most of the work."

"It really saved us," said Josh. "Yoni wouldn't have been able to climb a clothes ladder like the one Sari climbed."

"True. You were smart to think about the pole and rope ladder. You were—"

Josh wondered what Dana would say next. She'd said he was kind. She'd said he was selfless. Batman, thought Josh. Batman because of the cave and the fact that Roy had acted like his sidekick, Robin.

"Like Joshua," said Dana.

"I am Josh." Did she think he and Nate had pulled a switch again?

"I know who you are." She laughed. "I was thinking more of Joshua from the Bible, the way he led the army to scout out the land. You led the way to save Yoni and we all followed and helped. We were so organized. We worked quickly, and we succeeded! You brought out the best in all of us."

Before he could reply, the bus lurched to a stop.

"Everyone out!" ordered Gabi.

Josh climbed off the bus and saw a big banner stretched between two poles.

"It says, 'Happy Hanukkah,'" said Sari. "It's happy because you and Roy were able to rescue Yoni from the cave."

And Josh did feel happy, like hitting a home run the first time at bat.

"And the evening's just beginning," said Amit.

CHAPTER 21

Josh bit his lip to keep his teeth from chattering in the cold. They'd been standing in a half-circle for the last hour while people of different ranks gave long speeches.

Josh's legs were tired. He glanced over at Nate. His lips were blue too, but he stood straight, with his shoulders thrown back, pretending to follow every word.

Josh couldn't wait for the boring speeches to end. He was eager to get to the bonfire and the marshmallows that Amit had promised.

As Josh stood, his mind wandered. He thought back to how he'd felt when he first landed in Israel without a stitch of clothing of his own, and all his prized possessions on their way to Australia. So much had changed since then. Even Nate seemed to look at him with new eyes.

Sari shuffled her feet and stifled a yawn. Josh nudged her in the ribs. "You're not paying attention," he teased her.

"You're lucky, because you can't understand what's being said. If I translated the Hebrew for you, believe me, you'd be snoring away."

The others were stretching their necks to see above

the eighth graders standing in front of them. Nate turned, saw Josh, and gave him a thumbs-up.

The Scouts standing on either side of the banner were holding kerosene-soaked lamps that lit up the banner so that the words "Happy Hanukkah" blazed against the night sky.

"Wow!" said Josh.

Sari cheered. "Fantastic!"

"This year our Hanukkah celebration is a particularly special one," said the head of the tribe, switching to English. Josh leaned forward to listen. "As Scouts, we take an oath to help others, putting their needs before our own. And today, we have a new Israeli Scout who I think has proven his worthiness to become a proud Scout member."

Josh wondered who the lucky one would be.

"Josh, please take a step forward."

Nate put a hand on his brother's shoulder and shoved him. "Go on," he said. "You've earned it, brother."

Josh heard the round of clapping and slapping from his friends. He took a step forward. He no longer felt the cold. His heart was beating fast and his cheeks were burning with pride.

"Repeat after me," said the Scout leader. "I promise to do my best to fulfill my duties to my people, my country, my land, and to help others at all times and to obey the Scout's law."

Josh repeated the words as Gabi stood in front of him.

"The next time you come, I want to see this badge sewn onto your uniform," he said, handing Josh a Scout badge. Then he gave him a friendly punch on the arm.

"I promise," said Josh, stepping back.

"Hold on a second, I'm not done with you."

"You're not?" Josh looked over his shoulder at the others all standing at attention.

"And for your bravery, for putting the safety and needs of another above your own, we want to award you this Scout badge too."

Gabi took Josh's hand and placed the second badge into his palm. He folded Josh's fingers over it.

Josh clasped it tightly. He knew what was on it without even looking. All the other kids in the group wore the same badge on the pocket covering their heart. Like every Scout badge in the world, this one had the symbol of the lily in the center. But what made this badge different from the rest was the Star of David behind the lily, telling Josh that now he was one of them—a true Israeli Scout.